MW01147095

THERE'S NOTHING LEFT FOR YOU HERE

THERE'S NOTHING LEFT FOR YOU HERE

STORIES

ALLEGRA SOLOMON

FOUR WAY BOOKS
TRIBECA

Copyright 2025 Allegra Solomon
No part of this book may be used or reproduced in any manner without written permission except in the case of
brief quotations embodied in critical articles and reviews.

LIBRARY OF CONGRESS CATALOGING-IN-PUBLICATION DATA
Names: Solomon, Allegra, author.
Title: There's nothing left for you here / by Allegra Solomon.
Other titles: There's nothing left for you here (Compilation) | There is
   nothing left for you here
Description: New York : Four Way Books, 2025.
Identifiers: LCCN 2024035164 (print) | LCCN 2024035165 (ebook) | ISBN
   9781961897441 (trade paperback) | ISBN 9781961897458 (ebook)
Subjects: LCGFT: Short stories.
Classification: LCC PS3619.O43288 T47 2025 (print) | LCC PS3619.O43288
   (ebook) | DDC 813/.6--dc23/eng/20240802
LC record available at https://lccn.loc.gov/2024035164
LC ebook record available at https://lccn.loc.gov/2024035165

This book is manufactured in the United States of America and printed on acid-free paper.

Four Way Books is a not-for-profit literary press. We are grateful for the assistance
we receive from individual donors, public arts agencies, and private foundations
including the NEA, NEA Cares, Literary Arts Emergency Fund, and the
New York State Council on the Arts, a state agency.

We are a proud member of the Community of Literary Magazines and Presses.

"How clearly I have seen my condition, yet how childishly I have acted. How clearly, I still see it, and yet show no sign of improvement."

The Sorrows of Young Werther

"There is a loneliness that can be rocked. Arms crossed, knees drawn up, holding, holding on, this motion, unlike a ship's, smooths and contains the rocker. It's an inside kind—wrapped tight like skin. Then there is the loneliness that roams. No rocking can hold it down. It is alive."

TONI MORRISON

Beloved

CONTENTS

TRUE BLUE

People liked being friends with Alexandria because she knew how to shut the fuck up. This is what she always told Nikita—that was the difference between the two of them. The first time she said this was two weeks after the Tommy incident. The school's wound was still raw, bellying with consequences. She said it in her basement, game controller cold in her hands. Their adolescent bodies were lain on the hard carpet of Alexandria's floor, playing *Street Fighter* on the TV by the window.

It's a science, Alexandria said. You just soften yourself—cloudlike. You laugh not when the joke is funny, but when it's supposed to be. You smile and pout and bat your little eyes and say, *Really?* Never have an opinion. You are a "yes" man. You are kind and docile and dumb. They will pour themselves into you. It works every time. Alexandria began to bang on the controller.

Nikita watched the pale glow of the television screen bounce off Alexandria's dark face, mixing with the daylight. The sun was everywhere.

Right, Nikita said. You're better at it than me, though. People don't like me the way that they like you.

People don't have to like you, Alexandria said. That's what I'm here for. Her hand's quickened as Chun-Li took a sharp kick to Ryu's face, leaving him a red, panting mess on the ground.

Alexandria had always been exceptionally likeable—able to iron herself out, warm and thin, to soothe anyone that came close to her. Flatten herself into a non-threatening, doe-eyed, non-entity. People were loose-lipped around her. Felt warm—at ease. She played lacrosse in the spring and soccer in the fall, tightly knit with the teams year-round. She played the game well. Nikita did not. Nikita came to school and left when the day was over, leaving no trace of herself on the school or people. She did not play lacrosse. She was written up weekly because the plaid skirts, regardless of size, always seemed inappropriate on her body, in all the way it curved and protruded. She had huddled beneath introversion until Alexandria momentarily forced her out. This introversion was almost always interpreted as standoffishness. Which may be why in their freshman year of high school Tommy Adams told Nikita she looked like a bitch—that he'd never seen her smile. He said it outside the dining hall, right before bringing a hand to her cheek and pushing the corner of her mouth up with his thumb.

As the only black girls in their grade, they had gravitated instantly toward each other during freshman orientation. Nikita had just transferred from a school where there were at least five black girls—seven boys. Alexandria had gone to this school her whole life. Between them was a head nod, a knowing glance. Then, they'd become bound.

When Alexandria finished lacrosse practice, they went to Alexandria's home—playing video games or watching movies. Alexandria's mother and aunt lived together—always traveling as a unit. Their house had a perpetual, lingering smell of bread rising, with hints of mint from the plant in the kitchen. Mint would forever remind them of both of youth, relaxation, and safety.

One day, in October of their junior year, Alexandria came over to Nikita's house. They lay on the floor of her bedroom playing a one-on-one game of Egyptian Rat Screw. Alexandria was holding the majority of the cards when she said, You know, my mom lit a guy's car on fire once. Nikita looked up. Seriously? Alexandria nodded. My aunt's ex-husband. He wasn't good. That's why they live together. Alexandria had a very plain look on her face, as if this was all routine to her. My mom told me last night, she continued. She's done a lot of things like that, apparently.

I wish I could do that, Nikita said, putting down a jack before Alexandria put down a queen. I don't think I have that gene in me.

I do, Alexandria said.

They played until all the cards were in Alexandria's hand. She fanned them out over her fingers, before collapsing them smoothly. Then she said, Since I won will you tell me a secret?

Nikita let out a sigh. You already know everything about me.

Surely not.

She thought for a moment. Well, she began. I kind of like Tyrone.

I know that, Ki. Something else.

I got in trouble when I was seven for shaving off my eyebrows.

Alexandria was amused. Funny, she said. But no. Something else.

Nikita attempted to search for something else before settling on the obvious. This is when Nikita told Alexandria what Tommy said to her all those years ago. About her bitchiness. She'd kept it to herself.

He said that to you? Alexandria asked. Her face was stiff. Nikita just nodded and brought her own hand to her face, pressing a smile into her cheeks the way he had. It was the first time Alexandria went uncharacteristically quiet, pensive lines carved into her face.

The school pulsed the next day. A small chaos painted the glass walls of the junior lounge. Tommy Adams' girlfriend and co-captain of the lacrosse team, Lillian Barnes, was a whimpering, sobbing spectacle underneath the bleachers of the football field. Alexandria was there, rubbing her back— soothing her. When Nikita walked into the girl's bathroom, there, written in careful Sharpie on the mirror was: TOMMY ADAMS IS FUCKING AVA REYNOLDS ON THE SIDE.

The dean implemented handwriting tests a period later. Alexandria was never caught.

That night Nikita sat at Alexandria's feet. Alexandria had a rattail comb in her hand, dismantling the fraying black braids in Nikita's hair. Ava was a theater kid—something Alexandria also dabbled in—and she had drunkenly let the secret slip at a cast party, right before she blacked out. Alexandria told Nikita this as she undid the last braid.

When all the synthetic hair fell to the ground, the girls made ice cream sundaes. That's when Alexandria told her that the rush of it all—the chaos that followed, carrying out the act, hiding out in the shadows—it gave her an almost maniacal power. She felt like a god.

This is what began getting Alexandria up in the morning—that quiet havoc she could wreak. The slow, methodical collection of intel. Slowing wringing the life out of people, them not even knowing she was twisting them clean. She felt her body sharpening at all its edges. She told Nikita she wanted to become a deadly weapon.

Alexandria invisibly clawed her way through that school. Good behavior was rewarded, of course. She was just. She only disciplined those who had wronged her or Nikita. Alexandria was incredibly patient; understood the importance of timing. In fact, sitting on information for months made that moment of retribution more pleasing. People forgot she was in the room when they said something. Forget they told her something directly. Like the time one of Nikita's crochet braids slipped out and hung in the grass of the quad like a snake. Tyrone Harris, believe it or not, was the first to pick it up and swing it around. He made airplane noises and passed it to Steve Nelson, who passed it to Amy Scott, who passed it back to Tyrone. Nikita felt a pinch in the bridge of her nose and said, I think I'm going to cry, before heading to the girl's room. Alexandria could feel new depths being born within her.

The next week, Steve had people over while his father was away on business. The guilty parties were there. At four in the morning, when all the guests were sleep, Alexandria had let loose rats in the doggy door to his home. His ex-girlfriend had mentioned this access point at the lacrosse girl's lunch table once. Steve actually has a doggy door at his house, she said. I've never seen one of those in real life. Have you guys?

Parties became infrequent thereafter. If they existed, they had become clandestine gatherings.

At first, Alexandria felt bad about the innocents that got caught in the crossfire, but that was not something she could worry about.

Nikita was an observer by nature, almost entirely neutral about the morality of the acts, never getting involved. It seemed to balance—an eye for an eye. Humiliation for humiliation. Nikita's strength was her indifference, allowing Alexandria to act as she may. Cheering her on as she mastered different fight games after school. One day, while watching Alexandria play Mortal Kombat, Nikita said, I feel like I don't do enough for you. Alexandria banged on the controller, weaponizing Kitana until Sub-Zero was dead and gone. I don't need you to do anything for me, Alexandria explained. You're my best friend. You spend time with me. What more do I need from you? Nikita pulled a thread from the carpet. I don't know, she said. I don't want you to feel like you have to do all that crazy stuff for me. You can stop anytime you want. Alexandria paused the game and turned to her. One of her knee highs was around her ankle and the other where it was meant to be, right below her knee. It was always like that after a long day of school. The body, the clothes, disheveled. Ki, she said. If we don't protect each other, who will?

They decided after graduation they would stay together. They'd both gotten into Spelman, but Nikita couldn't afford it. So, Alexandria declined. They decided to go to the state school an hour from their home. At the end of that last year of high school Alexandria was valedictorian. She stood at the podium, black hair tickling the small of her back, and delivered her speech. I learned so much from this school, she said. So much that I will carry with me for the rest of my life.

Their freshman year of college they were roommates. Combined, they had about twenty articles of clothing in their closet. I've never not worn a uniform, Nikita said, pushing a finger through the knee hole of her only pair of jeans. I don't even know what kind of clothes I like. Alexandria sat by the window, taking a warm flatiron to her hair. I'll help you, she said. I'll tell you what you look good in.

Things were quiet that first semester. Making friends in college was more difficult than Nikita had expected. She had acquaintances here and there—people she said hello to in the communal bathroom, people she sat next to in class that made eye contact with her when things were funny. Nikita studied English literature and Alexandria did music production, so during the day they didn't see each other much. When they came home, they microwaved Velveeta macaroni and cheese cups, or piled pizza slices from the dining hall into to-go containers. One night, while watching *Dreamgirls,* Nikita said, I think things will be better next semester. Friendwise, I mean. I guess it just takes awhile. Alexandria nodded her head. It will be fine, she said.

The truth is, Alexandria did have friends. People she ate lunch with and studied with while Nikita was still in class. She got coffee with the same girl most Tuesdays at noon and they gave feedback on each other's songs. She still built bridges. It was in her nature—a siren will always lure. Regardless, she preferred spending her time with Nikita as it was.

That spring Alexandria joined a radio station club. They'd let local bands and musicians broadcast their talents once a month at a showcase in the school chapel. The reason Alexandria had become so fond of it, though, was because she got her own radio show. Every Thursday from 2:30 to 3:30 she had a slot where she exclusively played *Massive Attack* songs. It didn't matter which songs she played that whole hour—the first song was always *My Angel* and the last song was always *Protection.* On a Thursday that March, right around 3:20, Nikita lay on the red couch in the radio station, dragging her nails along the fabric to make a zipping noise. Alexandria played in the swivel chair and spoke as she introduced the last song. Once the mic was off and the glowing, red ON AIR sign was dim, she looked over to Nikita. Alexandria stretched her hand down into her backpack, pulling out a cow print notebook and holding it open to be seen. Every line was filled for pages.

What is that? Nikita asked, pressing her thumb against the pages, making it whir like a flip-book. Alexandria smiled and pointed to the topline. It's the library, she said.

Inside the notebook was every secret Alexandria had learned, starting on that day in October—the day Nikita told her about Tommy. It was the first secret she wrote down.

10/8 Tommy has been cheating with theater kid Ava. Lillian doesn't know

It progressed from there. Alexandria sat next to Nikita on the couch and watched her as she flipped through. She explained many of her favorite secrets. That upon finding out sophomore Penelope Smith was pregnant, the dean said she "could get that taken care of" or she "would be dismissed." That football team manager Layla McDonald had an obsessive crush on quarterback Travis Jones—would sniff his dirty jersey and rub his sweat all over her body before washing it. Lillian Barnes caught Ms. O'Donoghue and Mr. Miller after hours, fucking in the wings of the auditorium. The underground selling of pharmaceuticals, aided by Nathan King's doctor father. So on, so on.

Alexandria rambled on in her dream state as Nikita stiffened beneath her; shaken—not only that Alexandria had managed to attain this information, but that she was so meticulous—so serious—in regards to its collection. That she knew so much. As discreetly as she could, Nikita looked to see if any of her secrets were in there. She turned each page slowly, glossing over the fading ink to what appeared to be new ink, but there was no trace of her.

Of course, there wasn't.

After she closed the book, she said, You're so organized. This is amazing. Alexandria laid her head on Nikita's shoulder. Thank you, she said. Nikita held the book in her hands like something dangerous and fickle—as if the wrong turn could burn the whole radio station to the ground. I guess you don't need it anymore, then, Nikita said. But Alexandria just giggled, a genuinely humored laugh. What? She said. Of course, I still need it. Nikita went to turn her head but Alexandria's head in her neck stopped the motion. We don't even have friends, Nikita said. Nobody knows who we are.

That summer they were apart. Nikita got a scholarship to do a summer study abroad trip in London. Alexandria stayed in town and worked for one of her music production professors as a babysitter. Nikita felt a level of excitement to be apart—this excitement living in all the places guilt was not. She felt that Alexandria was, maybe, her only friend by default. Because she never tried with anyone else. But by the end of her trip, after the small, convenient friendships she formed dissolved into planes back home, she realized she missed her anyways. This was the most time they'd spent apart in years, and she wondered if it was the same dissonance twins feel when separated. A kind of raw vulnerability—as if the whole world has access to you when it shouldn't.

When she returned to campus, Nikita and Alexandria lay in the grass outside the library, talking about their summers. Before Nikita left, she had had this low, creeping feeling. Not that she was fearful of Alexandria, per say, but that she was wary of her. It had started that day in the radio station and carried into the spring. Sometimes she looked over at Alexandria in their old dorm, when she didn't know she was being watched, and tried to observe her in her most authentic state. She was just a girl. Sitting in bed with her red bonnet on—she was only capable of so much.

Nikita's shoulders hung loose—all the apprehension was released back into the earth with a breath. The sky was an ideal blue. Nikita told Alexandria stories of abroad and they both laughed; rolled around in the grass; their bodies sharp with happiness. The joy was almost claustrophobic. The sun set into a mix of colors, watery across the sky, and they stayed there. I'm so glad you're back, Alexandria said. I have so many people I want you to meet.

This year was about people. Time spent with them. Things shared with them. A joint pulled from one mouth and laid into another. Over the summer Alexandria solidified all of her radio show friendships and she brought Nikita along for the ride. Dionne and Itsuki were the heads of the station and had DIY bands play in their basement every weekend. Nikita often sat on amps and smoked while Dionne and Alexandria set up, plugging things in odd places. Strumming chords to test sound. Itsuki's band played whenever no one else was available, which meant his band played a lot.

This became the weekends. Sometimes the weekdays. Thrashing, screaming, passing joints through the confines of tightly packed rooms. Nikita went because Alexandria went. The times when she stayed home, she realized there wasn't much going on in her life when Alexandria and the many extensions of her were not involved. Alexandria made Nikita's life something she participated in, not something that happened around her, to her.

There was a night where they went to see a Pixies cover band play at Dionne and Itsuki's. The walls were slick with sweat. Alexandria was a body in hands far above Nikita's head before she was on the ground and back up again. Nikita's limbs were bending and turning. Her face in the damp back of the man in front of her. Sweat sour on her tongue, like something expired. Everyone's shirt was off. They'd all come off during "Tame." All at once, as if planned—like graduation caps. Alexandria appeared like an apparition in between the bodies. You okay? She mouthed one time. Her once straight hair had become thick and stringy at the ends, sprouting and sticking to her wet face. Nikita nodded. Then Alexandria was gone again. There was more bending, more falling. Nikita's body pretzeled left and right, before she stumbled out of the pit and on to the porch.

The bassist for Itsuki's band sat on the porch as well, half-naked in the same way Nikita was. His wiry body on full display. Collar bones protruding—something sharp invading something beautiful. It was autumn. Nikita sat next to Sebastián, her arms wrapped around her knees. The night sky consumed all the color of his face. Here, he said standing and heading to his car. I'll get you a blanket. Nikita watched him walk barefoot on the concrete to retrieve the blanket. It was the first time they'd ever spoken.

She had not ever loved anyone. It happened quickly with him, as she figured it would in that very moment.

After that night, before the love came, Nikita told Alexandria about their time on the porch. They were lying on the floor of Dionne's room while she was in the shower. Neither Sebastián nor Nikita went back in the house. They talked out there all night. David Byrne this, Andy Partridge that. Then, members of the 27 Club—who was in possession of a white lighter, who wasn't.

Nikita covered her face. His face was so close to mine, she said, muffled through her hand. I've practically kissed him. Her face hurt with optimism. She hadn't ever kissed anyone before.

Alexandria said that she'd been meaning to tell Nikita, but she lost her virginity that last summer while Nikita was in London. This made Nikita sit up straight.

What? Who? She asked her. Alexandria slowly ripped off a hang nail dangling from her pinky finger. I can't say. Nikita watched Alexandria looking up at her, basking in her curiosity—her desperation.

Are you still seeing him? Nikita asked. They heard Dionne's shower water stop. Alexandria didn't say anything and just laughed. When Nikita asked what sex felt like she happily volunteered that information. Dionne was back and joined them on the floor—Nikita helping twist her hair as Alexandria painted the picture. Alexandria climbed onto Dionne's bed, getting on all fours, and showing them all the many moves she'd done.

Your ass was not doing all that your first time, Dionne joked. Nikita laughed and fingered hair product into Dionne's hair. I believe her, Nikita laughed. Alexandria said thank you. This bitch is lying, Dionne said again. Nobody is doing all that off jump. They just aren't.

When Dionne left the room to use the bathroom, Alexandria told Nikita that sex was the closest thing she'd felt to retribution. And even then, it didn't come that close.

What does *that* feel like? Nikita asked quietly, barely over the air conditioner. Alexandria kept watch of the door. I can't tell you that, she said. It's like trying to describe colors you haven't seen. You just have to see them. Nikita watched her say these things with a bright grin. She realized Alexandria's having waited to say this when Dionne left meant she was not safe from her either.

Nikita and Sebastián's friendship developed rapidly; intensely. They sat together while he wrote songs and she wrote papers. He bought white lighters because it made her worry about him. She loved to worry about him. It was the perfect emotional foreplay. Nikita did not want to do anything that did not involve him. She went to bed thinking about him, dreamt of him, then woke up to his mental image, flickering absent in her eyelids. Thought of him at breakfast, while in class, while with Alexandria. Alexandria said the white lighter performance was white boy bullshit. That he'd watched a few too many Cobain documentaries and thought that dying young would make us all think him a better bassist in hindsight. Which, we would not. All Nikita said in response was, You don't think he's a good bassist?

Three weeks after that night on the porch, Sebastián played a show at Dionne and Itsuki's. The entire set he watched her. It was the best show he ever played. After, he pulled Nikita into a closet, picked her up so her legs were around his waist, and held her puffy hair in his hands. I can't do this anymore, he said. I need you.

She was no longer able to divide her time, then. She was entirely his.

His through the fall—through the spring. His all the way into the summer. Alexandria got Nikita in fragments. She slept at Sebastián's the rest of the school year—stayed at his family's lake house in Tahoe during the summer. She worked at a bookstore on the weekends and spent the rest of the time writing. They swam naked in the warm water and sun dried on the shore, dripping warm droplets on the books they were reading. He took Polaroid pictures of her bare body lying there at the edge of the water, embracing the sun into her desired, deepened darkness. Or, he filmed her on top of him, moaning his name as they fucked on that very same shore— trees and distant boats a mere thought in their haze. Pebbles and sediment finding their way into the crevices of their bent bodies. Your body is perfect, he often told her. I wish everyone could see it.

Nikita told Alexandria none of this. All Alexandria knew were the things she told her on the phone. Which was not much.

During the last week of them staying there, they invited their friends to come visit. Itsuki, Dionne and Alexandria showed up in a rumbling Jeep. Alexandria's hair was a bright brown, almost blonde, braided long and skinny down to her butt. She sprinted to Nikita in the kitchen and constricted her in her arms. I missed you, I missed you, she said. Dionne waited awkwardly for her to finish. Itsuki took everyone's bags upstairs with Sebastián. I'll go help them, Dionne said, already ascending the stairs. Alexandria excitedly pushed past Nikita and said, Show me the lake.

This was the first time Nikita had thought deeply about Alexandria in months. In that moment, she became aware that while she herself was doing things, Alexandria must have, too. She had not called her much that summer, and they had only texted in meaningless, fragmented bits.

Much like Alexandria herself, Alexandria's hobby was not on Nikita's radar. It operated in that same gray space that trees falling in the forest lived in—if she did not observe it, it must not have been happening.

In the middle of a different conversation, Alexandria said, with a certain edge, You know, the guy I lost my virginity to was Adian. Nikita's body froze suddenly. Like, Professor Thompson? The one you babysit for? Alexandria smiled and nodded her head. He was amazing actually, she said. Nikita didn't ask in what sense.

Well, he's married and everything, Alexandria continued. And he started feeling bad about what we were doing and said we couldn't see each other anymore. Alexandria stood up and walked towards the lake, slipping a foot in and letting the water creep up to her ankles. It's probably for the best, Nikita called from behind her, knowing it didn't end there.

Alexandria didn't respond to this and made waves with her feet. Do you wanna hear what I did? Alexandria turned to her with her trademark smile. Nikita's heart became tight. I don't know, she said. This made Alexandria frown. But it's good, she whined. Nikita put a hand behind her neck. The sun was setting into the horizon, glowing right above the distant line of the lake. Alexandria, was all Nikita said. It was quiet for a long time. Maybe ten minutes.

I started switching all his blood pressure medication with placebos.

There is not a timeline where Alexandria does not tell Nikita this information. She was very proud of this one. Nikita felt static settle into her chest. Goosebumps arrived on their own. Whether they were attributed to the air or Alexandria, she couldn't say. Why, Nikita asked, less as a question and more as a plea. Alexandria was still smiling. Ki, you're so boring these days. Is that what love does to you? If so, I don't ever want it. She then splashed some water onto Nikita. Nikita couldn't move. Alexandria, she said. Stop.

Alexandria rolled her eyes. That was all she did before stripping down to her underwear and plunging into the water.

At dinner that night Nikita watched Alexandria closely. The way she was silent while others spoke. The way she took in information with indifference. Itsuki told a story about growing up in Japan, all the things he got up to. Whenever it seemed he might say something secretive Nikita tried to interject. At one point Alexandria asked if she could use his phone to change the song that was playing. What's your passcode? She asked after he handed it to her. 1612, like the song, he said. Sebastián began singing the song and Itsuki joined him, not realizing what he'd done. There was nothing Nikita could do about that. While the boys sang, Dionne told Nikita that she had to go to the hospital the other day. She wasn't sure what triggered her allergic reaction. She checked everything she ate carefully for peanuts, but somehow she went into anaphylactic shock anyways. The two of them shared this in an aside at the opposite end of the table—no one else heard it. Dionne did not say more, but she looked at Nikita as if asking a question.

That night while Alexandria was in the shower, Nikita found the cow print journal and opened it. Alexandria had begun to cross out the secrets she used. There, crossed out with a date from the week before, was:

~~8/4 Dionne is allergic to peanuts~~

That was with a laundry list of other crossed out secrets. There was Adian's medication. Someone's work schedule. Someone's running path. She had been busy that summer—that was clear. Alexandria walked into the bedroom in a towel, body drenched in warm water. She didn't care at all that Nikita was looking in her journal. It amused her. I can tell you all about them if you want, she said, slipping into her pajamas. Nikita just stood with the book in her hands and pointed to Dionne's name. What did you do? She asked. Alexandria stood in one of Adian's oversized gray T-shirts that she'd stolen. She tucked her braids tightly beneath her bonnet and sat at the edge of the bed.

Dionne said you were a bitch for abandoning all your friends for a man. She asked me why I put up with you. Alexandria said this plainly. I don't like when people call you a bitch, she continued. I don't like when anyone says anything bad about you.

Alexandria's eyes were these vacant, round things. She did not offer this information with ulterior motive. She did not present it with emotion—she just told her.

There were many things Nikita thought about saying in this moment, but the sentence that won was: She's right.

She's a gossip, Alexandria said in a yawn, climbing into the bed. There was a deer head mounted on the bedroom wall and Nikita wondered if it foresaw it's slaughter before it happened. Nikita turned to Alexandria and said, I haven't been a good friend to you these days.

There are worst things in the world, Alexandria sighed.

Right, Nikita said. There are worse things. But I'm still a bitch.

Fuck you, Alexandria said. I love you. That's all there is to it.

When Nikita climbed in bed next to Sebastián, he pulled her by the hips. Had her lay on top of him. He dragged his nails up and down her back. I'm happy our friends are here, he said. She pulled one of his chest hairs between her teeth and said through a laugh, So am I. They sat there silently speaking through touch. Finger drawn lines on skin. A shudder, a slow sigh. Then she said, Sometimes I think that I love you too much. He laughed and it made his chest vibrate. How can you love someone too much? He let one hand begin to play with her hair. I don't know, she said. When you love someone too much you act recklessly. Sometimes I think Alexandria loves me too much.

Sebastián's hand on her back began to move slower and slower—began to linger. Alexandria isn't really reckless though? He said. If anything she's too friendly. It can be off putting at times, actually. Nikita made a note to never tell Alexandria that Sebastián said this.

Well, she continued. I've been reckless.

How have you been reckless?

I abandoned all my friends for you. When she said this, she could feel the very slow inhale and exhale of his chest, lifting her up, then dropping her. He did not deny it. Do you regret it? He asked. I don't know, she said. That's the problem. He had nothing to say to this either.

They remained like this. Sebastián's long eyelashes fluttering shut. The distant sound of water sneaking through the screen.

Do you think you love me too much? Nikita whispered. She listened closely on his chest for sounds of his heart's betrayal, but it did not waver. She turned her head to face the window and gazed into the moonlight. Her left ear was warm against his chest and she heard the machinery of his body whir. Sebastián said, I love you a lot, but I don't think I love you too much. I don't think you should put a limit on a thing like that. Why inhibit something that's entirely illogical as it is? Nikita nodded on his chest, and he felt it, like a small animal curling into him.

How would you describe it, she said. My feelings towards you.

His hands stopped moving all at once. This was before he brought his hand to her mouth, tracing her lips with his pointer. Religious, maybe, he said. It's like a kind of devotion.

She leaned forward to kiss his forehead, then the middle of his chest. His left shoulder. His right.

School returned late August. Nikita and Alexandria lived in an apartment complex across from Dionne and Itsuki's house. Sebastián was within a ten minutes walking distance in a studio all on his own. Alexandria found a new job giving tours on campus—the ultimate people-pleasing job. Professor Adian Thompson threatened a restraining order if she ever showed up at his house again. Sometimes she would stand across the street for the thrill—watch his small head bob in the upper left window. Dionne and Itsuki were in their senior year. Dionne spent most of her time working on her senior project. By default, this left Alexandria with Itsuki, which drew them closer. Alexandria began to spend free time holed up in Itsuki's room, learning the basics of guitar and talking until their eyes closed. Dionne busied herself.

Dionne never directly said she knew Alexandria was responsible for her trip to the hospital, but there was something in the way she interacted with Nikita after the incident. A trepidation that manifested in intentional word choice and, often, silence. There was a time when Nikita and Dionne hung out alone, doing work in a coffee shop.

What was your girl like in high school? Dionne asked. Nikita looked up from her work. Same as she is now, she said. Everyone liked her.

Dionne never brought her up independently again. Maybe because she didn't know how involved Nikita was or where she stood. All she said was, Hm. Then, went back to her work.

October of their junior year, Alexandria texted Nikita: Let's go to dinner tonight.

The girls found themselves at the Thai restaurant down the street, sardined in a booth in the middle of the restaurant. Alexandria ordered green curry and Nikita did the same. Alexandria's long braids were now red. Her nails were coffin shaped—long and black with white designs near the tip. Her eyeliner was a dull silver. While spooning food in her mouth, Nikita prodded Alexandria with questions about her day. The heat hit the back of her throat and made her cough. She asked, How is your new song going? And, How did your presentation turn out? But Alexandria's everything was on pause. She sat there nodding and answering as succinctly as possible. It was rare that Alexandria displayed any level of discomfort, but when it was present, it swallowed rooms.

Nikita saw the signs. The bend in her eyebrows, the focus on her surroundings. Alexandria knew she couldn't evade her much longer.

Alexandria, Nikita said. Say something please. Alexandria pushed around her green curry for a while. Perhaps it would make time slow. Alexandria looked down into her food and pressed on a loose bamboo shoot. I don't usually do this, as you know, Alexandria began. But because of the circumstances I felt I should let you know beforehand. Nikita felt the little bit of her food she consumed turn in her stomach. Let me know what? Nikita had not realized she said these words. They were produced more like a thought.

Alexandria dropped her spoon slowly and laid her hands in her lap, as if to say she was about to get to business. She took a deep breath and said, I intend to hurt Sebastián.

The waitress came by and refilled their waters. The girls did not break eye contact the entire time the half glasses were made whole. Even while the waitress asked, Is that good? They nodded into each other's eyes. When the waitress left and Alexandria didn't turn away, Nikita decided that, yes, this was happening. She watched a baby fist rice into its pink mouth across the aisle. A car ran a red light outside the window. A different waitress dropped plates in the distance, and the ceramic smack against the tile floor was one with this world.

Would you like me to say more, Alexandria asked. Nikita nodded her head slowly. Are you sure, Alexandria asked. Nikita took one long blink and said, I think I'm going to be sick. Alexandria touched her foot under the table. Do you want me to go with you to the bathroom? Nikita shook her head. Tell me first. Alexandria nodded and passed her phone across the table. It was open to a screenshot. She said, I found this on Itsuki's phone. When Nikita took the phone, Alexandria looked away and watched the same baby Nikita had been watching.

What Nikita saw was a group chat. The band boys and their brooding faces in tiny bubbles next to their names. Then there was a photo—there was brown. Brown skin and a blue sky. A still image taken from a video in which there was a parted mouth. A stretched neck and distant boats on the far side of the lake in the background. Dark areolas and tightly shut eyes and a girl in love with a mouth that could be letting loose a s-e-b, if she knew someone who possessed those letters, which she very well did. A face that looked as if to be taking in a tense anticipatory breath, like the one before someone sneezes, with light tears in her eyes, because that's how good it must've been. That's how good it was, she recalled.

The other members commented. She could not register these words. She did not want to.

At the very bottom of the screenshot, in a blue text bubble sent by Itsuki was: ya i wont be apart of this

Then: you have left this groupchat.

Since Itsuki left I couldn't see if Sebastián sent more, Alexandria said. Nikita held the phone in her hand, forgetting what it was. When was this, she asked. Alexandria played with her bracelets. I found it today, but it was from two weeks ago. Nikita nodded, as if this all made perfect sense. I'm going to be sick now, she said, standing up. Alexandria followed her. Down the hall, past the fish tank, into the girls room, into the handicap stall. Nikita got to her knees and threw up into the sterile white bowl of the toilet while Alexandria rubbed her back. Nikita's bare knees stinging against the tile. The image of herself on top of Sebastián from that low recording angle had tarnished the memory of that moment—Nikita no longer able to see it from her objective point of view. She did not see Sebastián's boney body laid on the lake's edge between her thighs. She just saw herself, paused in motion, loving him.

When her body was empty she sat up. Still on her knees, hands piously held in her lap, head bowed from looking into the toilet. She thought, this is what becomes of the desperately lost. This is asking position.

Nikita bent down further, looking under the remaining stalls of the restroom. There were no feet. She sat up.

What do you plan on doing to him? she asked warily.

I don't know. I have ideas.

When do you plan on doing this? Nikita asked again.

When I leave here.

Will you tell me what you do?

Alexandria shook her head.

Alexandria was at Nikita's side, sitting with her legs crossed beneath her, lower to the ground than Nikita was. Nikita looked down at her eyes. They were not anxious or assured—they were awaiting clearance.

If I asked you not to, would you not? Nikita asked.

Alexandria took a steady inhale, exhaled, and nodded her head.

In a strained voice, she said, In this instance, if you asked me not to I would not. If that's what you really wanted.

Alexandria looked soft, young, and yet she was capable of it all. Nikita saw it flash quickly in her eyes, the many things she had done on her behalf, and was still yet to do. She thought back to the day they played Egyptian Rat Screw—the day she first learned of the burning car. After she had told her about Tommy they had played another game. Nikita won that time, and Alexandria said, I would burn a man's car for you. Nikita laughed. I'm not sure if I'd want you to.

You would, Alexandria said, if he was a bad enough man. Nikita had figured she was right.

My mom and my aunt are untouchable, Alexandria continued. They're weapons. We could be like that. We could live practically forever.

I don't have the gene though, remember, Nikita said.

Alexandria had nodded and stuffed the cards into their box, before saying, It's just, I don't know what I did before you transferred freshman year. You're the only real friend I've ever had.

Nikita knew that Sebastián was right. This devotion, to be on the other end of it—it was sacrosanct.

They flushed the toilet and watched the vile innards of who Nikita once was spiral down into the pipes. They walked out of the handicap stall, out of the girl's room, past the fish tank, down the hall, back into their booth. Alexandria began to gather her things. Can I go? She asked. Nikita nodded. I'll see you at home.

THERE'S NOTHING LEFT FOR YOU HERE

I realized my neighbor was seeing the guy across the hall around the time things were getting rocky for them. Someone more astute may have put the puzzle together sooner; may have correlated the unvaried echo of the two doors closing. His, having freshly left her. Hers, after having watched him go. How one day their animalistic, guttural moans came crooning from my left, then directly across from me. It was electric the way their connection presented itself to me. The presentation itself was a slow crawl, but when it came, it was gleaming.

Earlier that year, I heard them arguing through the thin wall that separated my neighbor's unit from mine. My ear was cold against the plaster. I was addicted to this coldness; it was soothing, medicinal even. The argument wasn't a shouting match. It was coated in subtext—it was something quiet and brewing. Glimmers of the spat echoed to me—my neighbor's puppyish prodding, her boyfriend's stoic, male indifference—and then I heard the sound of her front door closing.

We're okay, right? he said.

She said, of course.

The interaction was almost lost to the white noise of my heater. It was in that moment I decided to take out my trash.

In the hallway, I saw him pushing her against her door with his hands in her hair as they feverishly kissed. A pink mess of lips and skin, missing the mouth more than making it. I made a note not to look at anyone too directly—to beeline for the trash room—but I have never been good at resisting temptation.

There it was: His black nails. Her shut eyes. I drank it up quickly, in one passive blink, and the afterimage of them burned behind my eyelids in a crisp orange outline. When the girl saw me coming, she squeaked a noncommittal plea of resistance that dissipated as soon as it appeared I didn't care.

It was quite the opposite; the two of them compelled me beyond belief. There isn't much else to it than this: I was awfully bored back then.

All my closest friends had moved out of state the year before, and none of us were good at maintaining emotional closeness over that much of a distance. My childhood best friend and simultaneous ex-boyfriend of five years decided that what we had was not a romantic love and never was. There were no good shows on TV and the Midwestern winter was a force. What else was there to do? I let my home swallow me whole.

In my boredom, I'd started to toy with the concept of reinventing myself. This was originally out of entertainment. Not appearance-wise. I more so wondered what would happen if I went against all my natural instincts and did what was thrilling rather than what I usually did, which was what was right. Act on impulse for any level of gratification without thinking of the effects, just to move my blood around. It wasn't always anything big. Sometimes I would steal candy from Walgreens and then throw it away because I could. Eavesdrop on my neighbors. Stare at people real long in public and watch them unravel before me. When I got delivery food I would either tip entirely too well or not at all, depending on the day and my mercurial temperament. It felt like I was grabbing my life by the neck and choking it out, deadpan.

Work had become the only social aspect of my life. I worked at Best Buy, recommending printers and televisions to fill the dead air. There was a guy I worked with named Josiah who would flirt with me in the breakroom—call me cute, short versions of my name while everyone else addressed me by every letter. Run his fingers up and down my forearms while we sat in the Nintendo aisle and argued about the most effective character to use in what game. His girlfriend was a nearly six-foot brunette. She lifted regularly at the gym and could kill me if she wanted, but—to her disadvantage—had the sweet, soprano voice of a *Sesame Street* character. She always picked him up at the end of the day or brought him lunch when her law school schedule allowed. I went out of my way to strike up a cordial friendship with her; ask her how the first year was going, make subtle jabs at Josiah to seem like a non-entity. Some days we would sit and talk for half an hour alone before she went over to him. On my birthday in January, she brought me a cookie with my first initial on it in icing. My complex relationship with her was one of my main sources of entertainment. The rush it gave me was too addicting to stop.

At home I would usually watch old episodes of *New Girl* or *Everybody Hates Chris* until my neighbors started up again. Some days my ex-boyfriend would stop by to collect some of his old things, but he always left quickly, without much word or touch.

Things with my neighbors became most enticing in February. There was a night where I heard the front door slam hard as they walked into the apartment; coming from—what I'd decided was—a dinner. I heard the bass in his voice, followed by the hard, undulating treble of hers.

I turned down *New Girl* and returned my ear to its home on that cold wall.

What about Christmas? she said. You wouldn't want to spend it with my family?

That's ten months from now, the guy said.

And?

And so, we don't have to worry about that right now.

You don't think we'll be together in ten months?

I didn't say that.

There was a soft, barely discernable whimper and then things were quiet again. I went back to my show and turned the sound all the way up.

I never heard the guy leave her house that night, or if he had, I missed it because my ex-boyfriend had called and asked if I still had his Cavs jersey.

Yes, I said, because you gave it to me.

He asked for it back calmly, and when I didn't say anything, he said, I'm kind of worried about you, by the way.

I laughed. Why?

Because you seem very lonely. Who do you talk to all day?

My neighbor.

Anyone else? he asked. You're not being self-destructive, are you?

Not yet, I said. Maybe it would be good for me.

I don't think that's true. You're a very logical and empathetic girl.

You worry about me a lot for someone who ended things.

He sighed.

Love is not exclusively romantic. I can still care about you. Quit isolating yourself—the pity party is getting boring. Then, he hung up.

The next day at work I realized I didn't really know what my neighbors' faces looked like, and I didn't know their names. This was exciting—it still is, remembering that mystery and what was possible inside of it. How my impositions still held water. I had just learned the girl had orange hair—I caught a glimpse in the hallway the night before. I knew the guy had jet black hair and pale skin, but that was all. Before I'd seen them, I had imagined them to both be blonds—that maybe they'd look eerily similar. They seemed like the type of white people to be attracted to a version of themselves. I imagined her apartment had pastel monograms of her initials on any bare wall space and a tank of ill-cared for goldfish. Through the wall my neighbor had the muffled voice of a petite, five-foot, stick thin sorority girl. In reality she was this tall, round, redhead with freckles. In terms of stature, the two of them looked each other square in the eyes.

Where's your mind at, Josiah asked. He was leaning back against a row of Mario games that avalanched onto the floor while he played with the hem of my polo. I was standing in front of him, spacing out into the open air over his shoulder.

I'm just thinking about my neighbor, I said, as though I was far away. She's dating the guy across the hall. I think they're fighting.

She your friend?

I nodded.

Relationships are complicated, he said. My girl and I fight all the time.

Because you're a cheater?

I'm not a cheater, he laughed. If I was a cheater, we wouldn't be standing out on this floor right now.

Josiah held my eyes for a long time before I broke the gaze and poked his chest.

I like your girlfriend, anyways.

Right. You two are all buddy buddy now. What's that about?

I don't know, I said. I could feel him affectionately tugging on my shirt as I began to disappear into my mind. I think it makes me feel powerful.

He flashed his teeth, laughed, then said with a mix of edge and intrigue, Most people wouldn't admit that.

I came home later than usual that night, having been stuck in traffic. Typically, the guy across the hall went to my neighbor's place around eight, and I was afraid if I was late I would miss an essential storyline. There had been many. A pregnancy scare, a forgotten birthday, unmatched love languages. (I wish you would compliment me more, she'd said once. I just told you that your earrings look cool, he said.) The pregnancy scare made me celibate for weeks, though, I suppose that had less to do with agency and more to do with the way things just were. When she forgot his birthday it wasn't a big deal, but it was obvious to me, a room away, that he was downplaying it. One time he waited in her house while she was gone to the store, and he talked on the phone to one of his friends about it. (Yeah, we didn't do anything, he said. No, no, it's not a big deal. You know I'm not big on birthdays anyways. Yeah, it would have been nice but, you know.)

It was certainly a relationship forged by attraction alone, and the mess of this reality began to creep up behind them. Though, none of this was important. This was a matter of self; I did not want them to break up.

When I got to my floor, I could already hear them as I passed by her door to get to mine. Desperate sobs. Akin to the pregnancy scare sobs, but less existential—more heartbroken. Long, deep, drawn out—like being pushed out of a brass instrument. Underneath those sobs was the guy saying, Come on. Are you serious? You knew this!

I stopped in front of her door and pressed my ear to it—a high-risk urge much easier to succumb to than you might expect. I could hear much better out there; the sounds were crisp and alive, like I was standing in the living room with them.

You knew this. Like—I told you that at the start, the guy said.

I didn't know you were *still* seeing other people, though. I thought we were past that.

Her sobs got caught in her throat.

I am. I am, but I like you both. That doesn't take anything away from you.

I can't believe this.

Come on.

I can't believe this.

To be fair, I had assumed she knew. Occasionally when she wasn't home, I would hear him walk into his place, laughing along with a voice that wasn't hers. It was always so conveniently timed that I assumed it was an arrangement. Her heaving proved otherwise, but it was entertaining, nonetheless.

There was an abrupt sound of heavy footsteps and the telltale sign of a lock being undone. I slowly and as unpanicked as possible, walked to my door and began to put the key in.

The two of them were suddenly outside with me. It felt familial, though neither of them noticed my presence.

Go. She pointed to his door.

Oh my God.

I'm serious. Go play with your other toy.

At this, I went into my apartment, only to get a better visual through my peephole. That was the money shot. At first, I could only see him—his back pressed against his front door, and his arms spread eagle, grasping for a way out.

We talked about this. You know monogamy isn't for me.

Then go—be free.

She walked so she was standing in his face, forehead to forehead with him. They yelled at each other for another five minutes before she said, I'm done, and walked back into her apartment. There were her footsteps, the click of the door opening, the slam, and then nothing.

The silence that followed was the quietest it had been in a month or two. I lay in bed and watched the ceiling fan turn until the arms of it liquified into one solid circle around the lights. I stared at the lights until it hurt my eyes; the bright circles, blinking residually in my view as I assessed my room. I had already been through both *New Girl*'s and *Everybody Hates Chris*'s entire series respectively five and four times; there were no surprises left. There was nothing. Not even a drone of white noise or leaking faucet water. I checked my phone and I had no texts. Instagram was mostly people I didn't talk to anymore. One of my friends that moved away slid up on a story I posted about *Insecure* ending and said: I guess Lawrence can stay. I liked it and said: Girl, I guess. I scrolled through the rest of our messages since she moved away. They were all about as inconsequential as that. YouTube proved to be temporarily mind numbing, and I watched a video essay about Mark Rothko. When that video ended, I stared at my reflection in the black screen and traced the outline of myself in the collected dust.

I found myself knocking on my neighbor's door before I could think better of it. Like a quick flash—my knuckles were against the hardwood, and then she was twisting the knob.

Her face was all red—freckles disappeared in the tear stained, inflamed skin. A mane of curls cascading down to her shoulders.

Yeah? She looked me up and down.

Hey. I live over there.

She just nodded, prodding me for the point.

I'm sorry, I began again. I just wanted to know if I could borrow a tampon.

She broke an apologetic smile that was crooked on its left side. Her face fell in a way that seemed she was embarrassed of her brashness.

God. Yeah, sorry. Here, just, um—She opened her door and motioned for me to come in. What do you want—light? Super?

She lived in a one bedroom that mirrored mine. The bathroom was in that first hallway, and I scanned her place as she disappeared into it. There was none of the personalized monogrammed art I'd expected. No goldfish. In fact, the walls were mostly empty aside from a few stock Ikea paintings and one lone, practically vintage One Direction poster right above her bed. The apartment smelled of nothing—no candles, no sprays, no oil diffusers, which was so un-twenty-something-year-old-girl like I wondered if there was something wrong with her. There was one withering set of flowers on the kitchen island, but that was all. I decided I liked my version of her place more—it felt truer.

I'll take what I can get, I said.

What's your name?

She was rummaging through the cabinet under the sink, pulling out hair straighteners and hair ties alike. I told her what it was.

That's funny, she said. You look like one.

Then she told me her name was Darleen, and I told her she looked like one too.

It's supposed to mean Darling—loved one, she said. Which, I don't feel much like right now.

Mine means "Filled heart," I said with air quotes.

Accurate?

I shook my head. No. Not right now.

She walked out of the bathroom with three tampons—two light, one super. Her body was swimming in an oversized Mets T-shirt, as if it was nightgown. As she placed them in my hand, she said, I know you can probably hear us. Sorry about that.

Don't worry about it. Seriously. I put the tampons in my pocket.

I used to hear you, too, actually. That guy.

Ah. I nodded my head. Sorry.

No, it's okay. I thought about you, actually. I hoped you were alright when I noticed he stopped coming around.

There was a moment of silence that sat a bit too long, but it maintained a softness I felt could be useful to me.

It's that guy right? The one that lives across from me?

She smiled and nodded her head—still fond at the thought of him, despite everything that had just happened.

Yeah. It's a funny story, actually. Maybe I'll tell you sometime.

Sure. Thanks for these.

I walked back into my apartment and put the tampons in the box with the others I had.

For a while, it did not seem like they were going to get back together. Because of this, it was silent in my apartment for three weeks. This was bad for me—I needed them to occupy my mind while home. I started taking extra shifts at work just to stay out the house. I would hope to come home and hear anything—them laughing, talking, fighting, fucking. But there was nothing. My ex-boyfriend had stopped coming by because he'd effectively gotten back everything that he wanted—excluding the Cavs jersey—but would call occasionally. It was always out of concern; out of the platonic love we'd built since we were children. At some point I stopped answering him. It felt like the wrong decision to make, so I made it. The residual high satiated me for a while. I called some of my old friends a time or two, but it was always brief and mostly unexciting in the way things never were when they still lived in town. Podcasts became important to me quickly. After work, I would sit outside the store and watch the cars go by.

During the third week of silence, I burned my hand badly at work. I was heating up water in a mug to make tea, and while taking it out of the microwave, I spilled it all over me. The skin temporarily became flimsy and loose, and the pain reduced me to a child. Whimpering and jumping as I shook my hand, like I'd fallen off my bike and needed a kiss. A few of my co-workers helped me get ice until Josiah came in and said, You're not supposed to ice it. Here, run it under room temperature water. He took my hand in his and ran the water over both of ours like it was his pain too. We stood there like that—his thumb gliding over the inside of my hand, soothing it—until I told him I felt okay. He then sat me down and rubbed Neosporin on my palm. Nice and slow, to savor the moment. We didn't talk much. I sat still and let him take care of me. It was then that I realized I had not touched anyone in a long time. I had not kissed anyone, hugged anyone, had my hand delicately loved on. It was a sudden but alarming revelation—discovering I was willing to do anything for it.

There was not much else. I attempted to build a bookshelf. Picked up a poetry book an old friend posted on her Instagram story. I started going for walks. Any control I felt I had dwindled into a thin string I could hardly tie. I had a close call stealing a candle from Bath & Body Works. I wasn't able to sleep all the way through the night, even with melatonin. I lay in bed most nights and filled the absence with my mind. I imagined they were talking on the other side of that wall, or perhaps, they were talking to me. Those moments felt awfully normal.

In that forth week, Darleen knocked on my door. Her face was hardly visible in the overgrowth of her hair. When I opened the door she had a bottle of Cabernet in her hand, dangling like a weight. Before I could speak, she just said, I'm kinda drunk, so kick me out if you want—but I need to talk to someone, and no one is answering my calls.

I would have been more offended under different circumstances, but my need for company was stronger than my pride.

The girl scanned my walls inquisitively, walked right up to a candle I had burning and took a strong whiff—told me the candle smelled like "man."

It's fennel and pine, I said.

Fennel and pine, she repeated absently. Her voice was softer, and raspier than I remembered. She took her free hand to scratch her forehead and began to lazily walk through the room, picking up notebooks before putting them down—opening and closing the blinds like they were some kind of puzzle. She thumbed at the tape holding up a Sade poster over the couch, and I fought the urge to tell her to stop.

You're not busy? she asked, rolling one of my pens around the inside of her wine-stained fingers. I shook my head. Can I just vent to you? She asked.

Of course. I repressed my excitement.

Literally stop me anytime. She then sat down at the kitchen table and began tearing up.

She and the guy started seeing each other in November. He had knocked on her door to see if she had a bottle opener. He never gave it back to her, so a week later she went over to get it—*I had bottles to open too, you know*— and he was like, I can't find it. Here, come in. She sat at his counter, and they talked for two hours. I remember thinking he smelled like a forest, she said. Right after rain.

The opener was in the kitchen drawer the entire time. And then they fell into a routine. She said at the beginning he did mention he was seeing other people, though, of course, she assumed the openness of their relationship was for the time being. When they started seeing each other every day she figured she was the only one, and all those nights he didn't come home she thought he was out being a drunken man with his friends at bars.

He's been texting me, but I haven't texted him back, yet.

Yet? I sat up.

I know it's bad. I like him, but I don't love him. We aren't entirely good for each other, but sometimes you just take what you can get. You know?

I do, I said. I looked at her; body perched in one of my kitchen chairs, sipping directly from the bottle.

You seem to be coping with your breakup well, though.

I shrugged. I wondered how she would feel knowing how much I knew about their relationship or the role she played in the coping.

He was the last person close to me that still lived in town, I added, rocking back on the hind legs of my chair. All our other friends slowly got city jobs and moved away one by one.

So, what do you get up to now?

Nothing. I'm very bored these days. I try to find ways to entertain myself.

What's that thing people say? she said, in a bubbly, burpy giggle. The idle mind being the devil's playground?

She drank more of her wine, and I watched it fall down her throat in cartoon-like gulps. It occurred to me that this interaction might not be significant to her. Just drunken therapy to exorcise her thoughts on her boyfriend—I, the only person present enough to help her do so—and in the morning, this would all be a hazy half memory, which could be qualified as a dream.

I was a place holder. She was white noise. I suppose we all do what we must to get by.

I have this idea of hitting rock bottom and becoming a worse version of myself, to then come back refined, I said.

She stared at me blankly. Why would you do that?

It might be fun. Keep me busy. It's like playing a video game. Making all these bad decisions, but they're mine to make.

Okay.

It was said as a half thought—her mind was elsewhere. She set the wine bottle down on the kitchen table. It was mostly empty and left a nice red ring on my white tablecloth. Then she said, I think I'm going to take him back soon.

Even if he's still seeing that other girl.

She nodded.

I'll just deal with it. I'm not good at being alone. Does that make me a bad person?

I'm not the best person right now, so you're asking the wrong one.

You keep saying that. She drunkenly tilted her head to the right, and it made her whole body sag a little. What do you mean? She asked smally. Like, what are you doing?

I mean, I sighed. I might fuck my co-worker.

That's not bad.

He has a girlfriend, though. And she's really nice. I like her.

Oh.

She squirmed a bit in her chair and averted eye contact. I realized that maybe her version of a bad person and mine weren't exactly mirrored definitions, but we were operating from the same core.

After a moment of silence, I saw her face tighten. She said, Please don't remind me of any of this in the morning, okay? Then stood up to throw up in the bathroom toilet. I could hear it echoing and splattering against the porcelain sides all the way from the living room. The retching was violent. I knew she would remember none of this the next morning.

I joined her on my knees, gathering her hair in my once burned hand like rope, and held her as her body lurched forward. After, I wiped her face softly with a towel, gave her water, and walked her back to her apartment. Inside, she climbed into a big sweatshirt—It doesn't even smell like him anymore, she said—and I laid her down in bed, pushing a trashcan to her bedside.

Lock the door, I called back. She said nothing.

Once back in my apartment, I wrote on a piece of paper: BUY HER FLOWERS. SHE WILL TAKE YOU BACK and slid it under the guy's door.

Work was slow the next day because there had been an ice storm. The roads were slick and empty, which gave us all free reign to be on our phones or take turns playing different consoles when our managers weren't looking. Josiah and I hung at the back of the store, standing as close as possible to the HD screens to see what it did to our eyes.

The thing is, I genuinely liked him as a person. He was dark-skinned, had a head full of hair, and was twice my size—which was just my type. Our humors aligned in a way he often told me his and his girlfriend's did not. I'm sure it was an intentional manipulation, but I didn't mind—it felt warm.

There was an high quality replay of a Steelers game unfolding before us. I was making a comment about how it felt like 4-D Smell-o-vision when he took my hand and used it to touch my hair.

You do it yourself? He asked, eyes not leaving mine once.

I smacked my teeth. Come on now.

He smiled. You know how do to cornrows?

Obviously.

He then took the hand and touched it to his head. I could feel the min-ute coils on my fingertips, already working themselves to burrow under my hangnails.

You think you can do mine? My girl's out of town.

I paused.

When? I asked.

Tonight.

Around that time, I often felt like I was suspended somewhere in the air, watching myself live and act and breathe. Observing my body move around powerfully from outside my body, like a video game—removed from my actions, my consequences. In that moment, I returned to my bones.

Except for Darleen, no one new had been to my apartment in a long time. When we walked in, I become hyper aware of the rolled up, dirty white mountain of socks in the corner by my vinyl—the way the couch frayed white where leather should have been. Where it once was.

Josiah walked to the front of the room and thumbed through a poetry book that was sitting on the TV stand, skimming the pages I'd earmarked.

Are you gonna show me around? He asked.

There's only two rooms, I said, more soft and less assured than anything else I'd ever said to him.

So, show me them.

He motioned me towards him. When I was standing in front of him he playfully turned me around by my shoulders and pointed to the painting above the couch. What's this?

I showed him the black and white Pollock imitation—left out that it was something my ex-boyfriend and I had worked on together, long before we'd even dated. I showed him the candles I hoarded and how they lived in the box under the TV stand, because I don't burn them faster than I buy them.

And this? he asked, picking up a golf ball sitting on my desk.

An old friend and I found it on a walk a long time ago.

You seem like a sentimental person, he said, earnestly in a breath. I shrugged and became very hot suddenly.

I have been one at times.

We walked onto my balcony and spit off of it onto the cement—it was his idea. He said he used to do that a lot in the place he grew up. A small apartment not too different from mine.

I felt it again then—a pinch of control while up there wielding our agency like gods. The pinch felt too much a moment later when his hand touched my back and he asked if we should wash his hair.

Yes, I heard myself say. There was an electricity in the air. A shift had occurred. I didn't have time to dwell on it. I was still trying to decide what kind of person I was.

We stood in the kitchen—he in front of me, back bent, head under the sink faucet. The room smelled like argon oil and mint—strongly gripping at the nose.

I used to love when my mom washed my hair like this, he said. And then, in the most airy, sincere voice I'd ever heard from him, I think this just brought back a formative memory.

I've never done this to someone before, actually.

I feel lucky, he laughed. To be your first.

My fingers were tangled in shampoo, washing and lathering his hair from the back, hardly able to reach over his tall frame. He laughed when I used my nails to really get in there. We were so close. I could see the open brown skin of his scalp and the way his hair sponged and soaked up the product. Something about seeing the top of his head, vulnerably caring for him in this way, humanized him to me. Proved he was breathing, warm to the touch, with blood inside. A person, with aches, hungers, memories. When he was a kid his mother washed his hair over the sink, and he used to spit off balconies—the facts of a real person with a real life. He was himself, and a son, and boyfriend. He was a boyfriend, and I was cradling his head softly in my hands.

When I asked if he okay he said, Yes—please, keep going. This feels good.

It had been more intimate than I had expected; the act of washing his hair and feeling the heat of his body alone in my home as opposed to the open exhibition of our job. It felt concrete, not just a playful, casual teetering on an awful edge for our own pleasure. It was clear that this could be the beginning of a consistent complication.

When we finished, I sat in a chair—he sat on the floor at my feet, facing the television. As time went on, I became quieter. Treading cautiously. I blow dried his hair as slowly as possible, attempting to find out if I was more moral than desperate, more selfish than kind, all while watching his hair go smooth in my hands.

When I clicked the blow dryer off, behind the sound of the television was my neighbor talking. There were two voices, dripping with the specific affection that comes post-reconciliation. She cooed and the guy laughed. I love them, I love them, she said loudly, and I wondered if she wanted me to hear. Yeah? He replied.

They don't sound like they're fighting anymore, Josiah said.

Yeah, I guess they're not. She's weak for him. I ran the end of a rattail comb down the middle of his head to form a part. They probably shouldn't be together if I'm being honest.

Who cares? Everyone's just doing what feels best to them, he said standing up.

He turned towards me and asked if the part looked straight, extending a hand so I would stand up too. His eyes scanned me as I stood in front of him re-drawing the part, pushing some hairs to the side, avoiding the warmth on my face and what I'd like to do about it if I were, in fact, more desperate than moral. His shoulders and my forehead were level with each other. Suddenly, my face was being held in his rough hands, pulling my gaze up so we were looking at each other. I took the comb and adjusted all the zig-zagging parts, making it as straight as possible. He licked his lips.

Remember what you told me you weren't, I said, quietly. At work that day.

I do.

What are you now?

In this moment? He laughed. I'm still not.

It just seemed like in that moment, us being out on the floor was the deciding variable.

I suppose you're right.

Josiah and I stood in a charged silence, and then he added, You don't have any roommates that are gonna come knocking, right? I shook my head. Any friends that just show up?

No, I said. No friends that show up.

Boyfriend?

No, I said. No boyfriend.

He nodded as his hands travelled cautiously to my lower back. Josiah's lips brushed against my neck as he leaned down to my ear.

That power you felt, he whispered. Do you still feel it?

His fingers pressed into my back slow and soft, as if playing a chord. My body knew that movement. It hummed. I exhaled as he inhaled, and I felt it as one.

To be honest, it all happened very quickly. I couldn't bring myself to speak—I just leaned into the touch.

APPETENCE

The woman arrived at the accommodation before the man did. She'd planned this. The woman had been aching for the occasion ever since the day she accepted the terms and conditions; her intrigue swelling taut and round with the passing days, awaiting puncture. She described this ache to her best friend a few days before as a kind of hunger. She said it strained her in the same anticipatory way a craving does, but also the charged, erotic tension preceding intimacy. It was a provocative kind of longing.

This friend watched the woman—a smile tugging the corner of her mouth, and said, It seems you have no interest in genuine happiness anymore.

It hadn't been that simple. It just so happened that over the course of those last three months, the woman had finally come to terms with who she was and what she truly wanted.

The accommodation was a condo at the end of a long street of identical condos. It had white trim and an emerald green Tuscan front door, wet and animated from the rain, like something oozing. Black porch lamps hung on either side of the door, equipped with delicate Edison lights. And then there, beneath the lamplight was a large, sleek, black box that said in bold letters: FOR "RUTH."

The man's box was next to hers, still waiting for him to come pick it up.

Inside the accommodation, the woman found the bedroom. It was on the ground floor with an adjoining bathroom. A candle was already burning, lit what only could have been ten minutes before by the organizers. It was vetiver. Ruth loved vetiver.

The woman brought her box in from outside and sat with it on the cold tile floor. There, she flipped open the lid and began to take out its contents.

A black bobbed wig, black press on nails, brown eyeliner, perfume, a silver chain necklace, a black slip dress with an intricate lacy neckline, black stilettos, and silver earrings that dangled in the shape of raindrops. Beneath all of it was a paper titled "RUTH" with the following:

[Note: These are all suggestions. You are not obligated to any of this. You may leave whenever you'd like. However, it is <u>heavily</u> suggested you do not share your real names for immersion purposes. The exit code is "Shangri-La." If either of you are to say this, the occasion is through and there will be a partial refund.]

The following details from your previous emails have been made readily available for you here.

RUTH: Black hair. Freckles across the nose. Perfume applied only at the back of her neck and her ankles. Short hair. A soft whisper for a voice—

It went on. The woman already knew these things. She stood to look at herself in the bathroom mirror. In the dim light, she saw her brown eyes and dark brown skin—collar bones protruding with her good posture and a mole on the inside of her left arm. Hair tightly braided down the back of her head in precise, neat cornrows. A timid smile pulled at her— she watched the gentle rise and fall of her chest before stripping down to bare skin, then building herself back up, making herself anew. She dotted brown eyeliner across the bridge of her nose, dusted the perfume in the allotted places, and then made her way to the living room.

The woman sat for ten minutes, heart in marathon. Insides feverish. She heard the sound of a door closing somewhere in the house and straightened, remembering.

Ruth has good posture. Ruth doesn't smile with teeth. Ruth is forthright, praising, and physical.

She unfurled her hands slow, preparing them for touch. As she did this, the man came down the stairs and looked at her.

He had dark skin and short black hair faded at its sides. He wore a red button up with the top three buttons undone and the sleeves pushed up to the middle of his forearm. The gold necklace was there. There was the same confident, assured gait. Both of his ears were pierced with small gold hoops, and the woman wondered if the man had already had those piercings beforehand.

He was wearing the shoes. He smelled the way he was supposed to.

The man looked at the woman as if she had hurt him.

Ruth, he said, with zero conviction—eyes looking through her.

Yes, she said. She watched the vacancy in the man's eyes diminish slightly. You're perfect.

Thank you. She paused, then walked toward him, slow and careful. The woman hesitated before reaching to hug him at an unassuming pace. They held each other, and the embrace tightened as her nose pressed hard into his neck. Nose squishing into a mound, engulfed in Tom Ford cologne. There was a bite to the soft scent that routinely undid her.

James, she sighed in a shaky, affecting breath. When she pulled away her eyes were glossy and fanciful. She repeated the name again, then told him he had done a wonderful job.

Thank you. He took a step forward and set his hand gently onto the small of her back while placing a kiss to her forehead. Should we head out? He asked.

Everything unfolded as they were told it would. The man and the woman headed to the car and the man drove them to the first part of the night.

Ruth, the man asked, what have you been up to? The woman adjusted the bangs of her wig with her pointer finger and touched the man's thigh as he drove. She could feel his firm muscles beneath the fabric. He had the exact physique.

The woman said that she had not been up to anything, really. The man asked if he could tell her how his day was, and the woman said yes. This was his time after all.

He drove them through downtown. The streets were wet with rain and made the reflection of the stoplights like watercolor. The man stated that he had made partner at his firm. The woman squeezed his thigh at this news and kissed him on his cheek.

The man looked at the woman.

Thank you, he said. There was a tonal shift in his voice, and then he returned to talking about his life. The move. The old house had roof problems, and he saw no use funneling money into it when he could find a nicer place. She nodded along and said that made perfect sense; hand on his hand then, stealing warmth.

They made it to the restaurant. It was a small, reservation-only seafood place tucked into the back of a garden. He walked to her side of the car and opened the door for her, gently holding her. The woman had been told Ruth enjoyed pampering like this; being treated with classic affection. Held doors, letters, flowers. The woman related to this and made a point to show the satisfaction in her eyes. To please the man.

Even so, for a moment the woman closed her eyes and allowed herself to just smell the man. The familiar bite of the cologne. Feel the rough grooves of his hand in hers and picture whom she wanted to picture. Only for a fleeting moment, then she returned Ruth back to him.

When the time came, he ordered for them both. Sea bass for himself, ponzu glazed salmon and sticky rice for her.

I hope that's alright, he said candidly as the waitress left. He placed the cloth napkin in his lap.

Oh, that doesn't much matter. She smiled.

It does, he said. Of course—I understand what you mean. But it does.

The woman regarded this affair with a level of seriousness she didn't allot most things. She figured to get what she wanted out of it, an extreme attention to detail would be necessary. Ahead of this meeting the woman had watched two of the man's favorite films.

I've watched this one about twenty times, I believe, the man said.

Is it your favorite of the two?

Maybe. I think so. He chewed and the sea bass congealed with the white of his teeth. Jim Carrey is brilliant in it.

Is that why you like it? These are both Jim Carrey films. I didn't know you loved him so much. The woman talked low and soft. Ruth loved salmon, so she savored every bite.

I do like him a lot, actually. The man took a sip of his drink and then sat so his back was firmly against his chair. I think this one captures nostalgia accurately, and the pain of it. That, and it's always made me want to go to Montauk.

You should. Why haven't you?

He shrugged and wiped his mouth—sea bass now gone. I don't know, he said. I think I believe that if I go something interesting will happen to me. Like I'll have some sort of epiphany or finally be in the right place at the right time. But I know it's just a place, and I would go and probably feel nothing.

I don't think that's true. How often do you do something and feel nothing at all?

I don't know. He looked at the woman for a moment then played with his side salad.

Should we go up together sometime, Ruth? He said this without looking up from his food.

Yes, the woman said. Why haven't you asked me before? I'd love to.

Alright, then. I'll plan for it.

The waitress came back to ask about dessert. She was a tall stick-thin brunette with perfectly placed freckles. The man's eyes lingered on her for a moment before ordering a carrot cake for the two of them to split. The woman touched the man's foot with her foot under the table. He flinched for a moment before relaxing, letting it rest there for the duration of date.

When dinner was over it had begun to sprinkle again, and they did their best to sprint to the car. It was a light rain that turned dewy on the skin.

Between that dew and the soft light from the lamps overhead, the man thought the woman looked beautiful. He thought Ruth looked beautiful.

Once in the car, the man touched the woman's face, held it in the space of his right hand—her chin pressed against the fleshy pad of his palm. Ruth loved having her face touched. She loved being handled. The woman had been told that it made her feel precious and delicate, like glass, and the woman found that she was right. It was electrifying to be treated with such fragility.

I want to kiss you, Ruth, he said.

Kiss me.

You're sure?

Yes. Please kiss me. I've missed it.

The man leaned in and kissed her simply. There was a deep sigh while their lips were still connected, then he gluttonously reached for more. The man's hand slipped to the back of her neck and held her into him more firmly with his pointer and thumb. The woman kissed him back. There was vetiver. There was her perfume, her hair. It all worked together sadistically.

I've missed you so much, the woman said in the space between. I've missed you like this.

The man's body grew tense as he continued to kiss her, pushing the comment aside—grip faltering on her body.

You're so warm, the woman said. She slid her fingers into his hair and brought her hand down, rubbing his ear soft between her fingers—a gesture she'd learned she should do.

The man's lips stopped moving with an awkward abruptness, though their lips were still pressed together. He then removed his hands from her, grew the space between them, and sat back into his driver's seat.

Is everything alright? The woman asked.

He began to nod his head but didn't commit.

They sat in silence a moment. Then, the man reached for his phone and began to play Tchaikovsky. The woman didn't move, and she didn't look at him. She wondered if that was too much, but too much was exactly what she was going for. She assumed it was what he would've wanted because it's what she would want.

He turned to her after a while as he put the car in drive. The light of the sky bounced off his skin and made him a cool Prussian blue.

I'm all yours now, he said, as if the version of himself that was just there had vanished altogether. They pulled off.

This was her time. This is what she had ached for.

Once the car pulled off and they were far enough from their previous destination, the woman said that she'd missed him—James—and asked what he'd been up to. The man said not much, really. The woman asked if she could update him about her life and he said yes. The man had his hand on her thigh as she spoke, tracing circles on her exposed skin below the hem of her dress with his pointer finger at red lights. There was a danger to this she enjoyed—it made her entire anatomy sharp with nerve. It was one of James's best traits, she thought. That there was no end to his affection.

She told him that she'd changed jobs two times in the last three months before deciding to work full time on her poetry book. It's funny, she said, because you told me to do that a long time ago, and if I had I would've been done by now.

Oh, but you've gotten around to it, and that's all that matters. He planted a kiss on her hand and the turmoil in her chest returned.

They arrived at the observatory ten minutes before the show was to begin in the planetarium. The man and the woman sat outside on a bench. There was a family to their left with an infant baby, and a high school couple to their right so consumed by nerves they were too anxious to touch.

The woman took the man's hand, wrapped it around her lower back and then leaned into him.

You know, she said. All the poems in the book are about you, James.

You flatter me. The man kissed her ear.

Even though you never write about me, she teased.

The man forced a smile. I'll write something for you, love. I'll do it tonight.

Only if you want to.

I'll do it tonight.

The two of them exchanged small talk while they people watched.

Remember the first time we came here, she said looking at the high school couple, and we wondered how long it would take us to walk to the West Coast? You said if we were going to go to an observatory we should go to Griffith.

Yes, the man said flat. I do.

I think that would be an alright experience. Walking to LA with you. No cars, no trains, no hitchhiking. Just walking. She turned her head and closed her eyes, so her nose was in his neck again. His scent was all she ever needed.

It would take a lifetime to do, the man said.

That's the point.

It's also nearly impossible, he laughed.

You always loved logic. She pulled herself from his neck and squeezed his thigh. You've always loved logic.

Inside the planetarium, they made home in comfortable reclining chairs that trained their gazes upwards to the large black dome-like screen above them.

I've never done anything like this before, the man whispered to the woman in an earnest confession. And then suddenly after, Sorry.

No, it's okay. I hope you enjoy it.

The video started with loud orchestral music surrounding them from all sides. The screen began to take them through the solar system; expanding the more they strayed from earth.

You see, the robotic narrator said, once they'd passed the dwarfed planet Pluto, we're here, and we've only just begun. The screen began to travel out into the dark expanse of space, the arrow pointing to earth disappearing into miniscule darkness. The man squeezed the woman's hand.

When we put things to scale like this, it's hard to return to your daily life, no? The narrator said again. We are insignificant specks upon insignificant specks floating around in space.

They traveled deeper into black matter and at some point, the woman wasn't sure when, the man let go of her hand. The show was thirty minutes long, and once it ended it seemed as though the entire audience was disoriented; reminded of the smallness of their humanity in a universe too large to comprehend.

When the woman sat up, she looked over to the man. He wasn't moving.

James? She said. The man didn't budge. She moved closer to the man and touched his hair. Hey, she said. Are you okay?

The man closed his eyes then opened them.

He said in a broken shudder, This is very hard.

It was soft and strained, then he made his way to the car without checking that she was in step.

The two drove home in silence. The woman took the wheel as the man looked strictly out the window, now and again passively giving directions to assist in getting her back to the accommodation. Whenever she got a moment, she would steal glances at the man. Watched the way his hair curled tight at his scalp and disappeared into shadows around the sides of his head. There was a scar at the center of the back of his neck, and every breath he took was an audible one. She did not know this person.

After she put the car in park in the driveway, the overhead lights came on, and she saw a slight red tint on his ears where the piercings were. They were fresh and swollen: new.

You want to stop, the woman said suddenly, almost defeated. They were sitting in the quiet of the car, neither of them getting out.

He shook his head.

Are you sure? She looked over at him and his hands were crossed over his lap, fidgeting with the rings on his fingers.

Just give me thirty minutes. He stepped out of the car and into the accommodation.

The woman waited in the living room. There was a vintage dresser in the corner with a record player atop it—an ornately detailed full-length mirror to its side. The woman looked at herself. The black hair. The hugging dress. The faux freckles across her skin. She thought, I will never be this person. And then: I am having the time of my life.

She filed through the records, looking for something that spoke to her. The winner was DeBarge's 1982 album *All This Love*. She let it spin and lay down on the green velvet couch.

The man returned a few songs in, as "I Like It" played. He stood in the hallway leading into the living room; hands in pockets, earrings out of his ears.

I like this one, he said, with a voice and affect she hadn't heard all night.

The man began undoing the buttons on his shirt in the name of comfort. The action was devoid of all sensuality.

Me too.

You can take that thing off, if you want.

What? She sat up.

The wig. He motioned to his head and did a playful, defeated laugh. Feel free to be done with it.

Okay. She took the wig off with a reserved, slow hand, revealing her short black cornrows beneath. His eyes assessed her in a way that felt reminiscent of the way she'd assessed him in the car; becoming acquainted with her humanity and personhood, with all the small details.

Do you want to stop, she said, holding the wig in her hand.

No. You keep asking that. Do you?

Not at all, she said. But, the wig.

Yeah, he sighed. I want to try something different. I'm sorry about earlier. The man poured himself a glass of gin at the bar cart, then took a seat next to her on the couch.

That's okay.

I feel I may have ruined the experience for you. You were an expert Ruth, by the way. The best I've had. He touched a friendly hand to her shoulder and then took a sip from his glass.

How many have there been?

Fifteen before you. My savings are drained. Then he said, with a crooked smile, It has never been as horrible of an idea as it has been tonight.

She laughed to herself—proud of this. Why's that?

The man took another sip of his drink and played with the jewelry on his wrist. You were so much like her, he said. It was horrifying.

The woman watched him jitter—heard a subtle break in his voice before he smoothed it out.

In the car when we kissed. When you said those things to me…he shook his head. It felt like you took a butcher's knife to my throat. The man began to take the jewelry off and place it on the windowsill behind them. The overhead light flashing onto the gold caught her eye. And in the planetarium, he said, seeing everything being put into perspective, seeing our insignificance put to scale only made me care more. If everything is so insignificant, if we are specks on specks on specks, why not find someone that makes you happy and cling to it?

That's what we're doing, isn't it? The woman mused. Taking what made us happy and clinging?

The man leaned his head to the side and looked at her with an expression she couldn't decipher. He then asked the woman if this was her first time using the service. She said yes.

He asked her how long she and James had been apart. She said three months.

What's your name?

She looked at him.

We won't end the night. Tell me your name.

The DeBarge record had gone quiet, expelling a soft sifting sound, begging to be flipped. As she stood up to flip it, she said Jamila.

Jamila, he echoed. Ruth and I have been apart for two and a half years.

She repressed a soft smile. It was all so exciting.

What's your name? she asked.

Wren.

She nodded her head. Do you want to change?

Wren brought his box to the bedroom, and they both rifled to the bottom. At the bottom of his box were silk black boxers, a silk black button-down shirt, and—what they assumed was the alternative—a large white T-shirt with the name of a band he'd never listened to, and plaid pajama pants.

Out the corner of Jamila's eye she caught a glimpse of Wren's sheet in his box—all the details she submitted to the organizers. It was odd seeing James dwindled down to key phrases—a person reduced to text—but there was even excitement in that oddity. That wretchedness made her feel like a real human being.

Remaining in Jamila's box was red lingerie—sheer lace thigh highs that stopped right above her knee. Garters. Underwear that was entirely translucent and a bra constructed only with push-up technology in mind, not comfort. Then, her alternative—a baggy white T-shirt and Nike running shorts.

Wren went for the shirt and black boxers, a compromise. Jamila went for the shirt and the underwear. He went into the adjoined bathroom and began to dress himself in the mirror with the door ajar.

A point will come when you see this is all useless, Wren said as he undressed. You're still eager. You still think this is an adequate substitution, but it's not.

What else could it be? She lay back onto the bed, into the pillows, and pulled the shirt over her head.

It's masochism.

Wren pushed his shoulders back to take off the shirt he'd been wearing all night, and through the crack of the door she could see the hard pulse—the muscular strain of his body as it contracted with his movements. The soft dewed skin on his back. She wondered what it might taste like to lick his back and what it might feel like on her tongue. If it would taste horrible, in turn making it terribly thrilling. For a moment she closed her eyes and could smell his sweat doused cologne—feel the small strands of his body hair in her teeth—and then it all came rushing in.

She wished they hadn't exchanged names, that he was still a nameless vessel of desire.

He came out of the bathroom, turned out the light and sat next to her on the bed. He saw the way her eyes watched him, full of intrigue.

Does this not hurt you, he asked.

Jamila closed her eyes and wrapped a hand around his bicep. His skin was soft and everything inside was firm. She leaned her head on his shoulder and took a long inhale. A long exhale. Then said, Smell is the sense we most associate with memories. Did you know?

Is that true?

Yes. Come here. She took his head and brought it close to her neck. Breathe in, she said. He did as she asked. She could feel the soft shudder of his body against hers.

God.

Wren's arms found her waist and tightened.

Again, she whispered, as she did the same.

Wren obeyed and felt his heart nosedive.

Jamila, he sighed, almost in a plea.

Ruth, she corrected.

Their lips nearly found each other. Before the point of connection, Wren pulled himself away, sat pensively at the end of the bed for a few seconds, then went into the bathroom. She waited for him. He stayed there for ten minutes. She heard rushing water. After, he appeared with a dewed face and invited her to the backyard to look out at the dim horizon.

*

Ruth was a teacher, Wren told her. The sky was graying and they sat in chairs on the back patio. He said she didn't enjoy teaching that much, but she was good at it. She was constantly at odds with herself because of this fact. Wren did not ever make partner because he was not a lawyer. He had never been a lawyer. He and Ruth would occasionally make up storylines for themselves in the car on the way home from work. Wren worked in construction.

There was a day, Wren began, it was one of the last good days, where we talked like I was a lawyer and I made partner, and she was a film director, and she got a standing ovation at Cannes. After the conversation we went home to our one bedroom and were brought back to reality.

Wren wouldn't look at Jamila when he talked.

Maybe I'm here because I have pre-existing conditions, he said. I've always enjoyed pretending.

How'd you afford the service so often working in construction?

I sold all of the things she didn't take when she left. He nervously scratched behind his ear. And I had the money I'd been saving for a ring. I wasn't joking earlier, he laughed. All my savings are just about gone now. I'm affording this one on a payment plan. It'll take a couple months to pay off.

You must enjoy yourself here then. The two locked eyes then and she saw the brown of his eyes was lighter than James's.

A little, he said below his breath. Never for long.

Wren's voice reminded Jamila of something natural; rough while sooth-ing, like sand.

The first time, he said, I was so nervous that I said the exit code ten minutes into the first half. We were at a movie and I walked out

sweating through my clothes. Wren crossed his ankles. I actually ended up seeing multiple of the women I met through the service on the
outside for a while. One of them I dated for about two months, but we
couldn't escape the fact that neither of us was who we really wanted, so
we ended it.

Have you tried getting Ruth back?

She wouldn't take me back, he said. I don't have to try.

Wren said Ruth had disappeared in the night. He went out with friends
and stumbled into bed, drunk. When he woke, she wasn't there. On the
kitchen counter was a note written in green sharpie on a napkin that said,
I DON'T BELIEVE THIS SERVES ME ANYMORE. YOU HAVE
MADE A FOOL OF MY LOVE.

What did you do? Jamila ashed a cigarette and leaned forward.

I don't know, Wren said, soft and timid. His eyes a wandering mess. It
was quiet for a while, then he said, Well. I don't know what she knew.

So, you did do something.

I'm human.

Were you unfaithful, she asked.

Sure, he said. But we'd talked about it before. At least one of the instances.

Jamila coughed, smoke leaving her mouth. It makes sense now, she said.

What does?

She leaned forward and ground the remains of the cigarette beneath
her heel.

You have the pain of someone who ruined something good for them-
self. I don't think it would hurt this bad this far down the road if it hadn't
been self-inflicted.

I don't know if that's true.

It is. It's a specific type of agony. It's the same pain as mine. She folded
her legs so she was sitting crisscrossed on the chair. Ruth is probably fine.
Even if she loved you, she's probably okay now because it's not weighing on
her conscious in the same way.

Fuck you, he said in a dismissive, quiet tone. You don't know anything.

James is fine.

You don't know anything.

I'm not trying to upset you.

You're miserable.

The woman smiled, amused and unaffected. We're both miserable, she said. That's why we're here.

There was a heavy wind coming in. Jamila watched Wren turn away from her and let the wind hit his face, hard and invasive, like it was molding him.

Thirty minutes went by. It was fully dark then, the patio only lit by a string of backyard lights and the living room window behind them. The air smelled of petrichor. Wet and earthy, like rebirth. The wind picked up and began pushing their clothes hard against their bodies, making all the divets and protrusions more evident. Their bodies were a spectacle waiting to be beheld. They both did their best to not look too hard at the other.

There was an anxious anticipation within Jamila. She was still eager. She did still see this as an adequate substitution. She looked over to Wren who was looking over at her; thumb playing with the hem of his shirt.

Jamila asked Wren if he had ever heard of stress-induced cardiomyopathy. He had not. She moved closer to him. She told him she looked it up after the breakup because she felt like she was dying. When she explained that it's nicknamed "broken-heart syndrome" and that it can be caused by extreme emotional stress that weakens the heart, Wren said he may be in the beginning stages, and that maybe his heart will soon run out of steam.

Too much time has passed, Jamila said to him. You'd be dead by now. I'm still at risk, though.

Three months is also a long time apart, Wren said. They were closer now and sharing Wren's drink. Why are you still alive then?

My pain grows every day. I haven't reached my peak. She took a sip of his drink and swore she could taste hints of him.

So does mine.

I bet you love it, she said.

The pain? He asked.

Yes. I bet you love how wretched you feel.

Wren's face contorted; less out of intrigue than of genuine offense.

Why would you say that?

Because, she handed his drink back to him, it feels profound. The thought that anything could make you feel that awful is validating. That it must've been love. She looked at him, waiting for him to disagree, but he went on staring at her, dazed.

She continued. When you feel miserable, the sensation is so intense that it feels like death. When you're happy the feeling is so light, so subtle. Almost trivial. That's how I feel. She scooted closer to him and laid her head on his shoulder. His skin was warm through the fabric, comforting her cheek.

You love being miserable? He asked.

Don't say it like that.

Like what?

Like you don't too. Most people do.

I don't, Wren said. Jamila's head was in his neck, but he didn't move. He inhaled her perfume as she did his cologne.

Why haven't you moved on then?

I don't know, he said. Guilt, probably.

So, you want to torture yourself about it forever? It's been two years. Forgive yourself. Find your happiness, she teased. Go cling to it.

Wren didn't have a response to this. Jamila reached her hand up to his head and began to drag her black nails through his hair. The muscles in his body relaxed as he leaned into her.

James was the only person in my life that had ever loved me, she whispered.

Is that true? he asked, mind drifting with desire.

Jamila nodded. It was the most secure I felt in all my life. Everything felt too easy. She pressed the flat part of her fingertips into Wren's scalp and began to massage his hair. I remembered, she continued in a quiet breath, how intense every passing moment was when I was begging people to love me. When I was constantly on edge; pining for years after one person. That tightness in my chest before bed, the constant anxiety—I didn't feel it anymore. She closed her eyes. I always felt so alive in that misery. It felt as if that intensity was the purpose of everything. Being moved like that.

Wren shook his head. I don't believe you.

Believe what?

That you actually think that. You just want to be interesting, and you want me to be interesting with you.

His hand was on her thigh now, the pressure inside the grip growing with the passing moments.

I really did. I still do. That's why I ended things with him. She blew air out of her nose, slightly amused. It didn't take longer than a week for me to realize that was the truest love I would ever feel in my life, and it would be forever thwarted because nothing felt real if it didn't feel terrible. It's an unfortunate truth, but it's my truth. Jamila took a hard breath. It's hard to explain, she said. But it doesn't really upset me anymore.

Wren ran his hand up and down her thigh. You do torture yourself.

It isn't torturous. She nuzzled further into his neck. The opposite, actually. I feel alive because of it.

It was silent for a while between them. Wren eventually kissed Jamila's forehead and then ran his fingers through the parts in her hair.

There have been times, Wren admitted, that the agony of missing her is so strong I believe it will stop my heart.

Does it feel good? she asked.

He pulled Jamila up by her chin, put his head in her neck, inhaled, and sighed. I don't know, he said. Maybe. It feels like an important love.

It's not love you're after, she said.

I don't want to think like that. I don't necessarily think that's true.

I had a nice time with you.

Wren looked at her and nodded but didn't verbally agree.

They sat there huddled into each other's bodies breathing with a quiet hum that was usurped by the sound of the weather around them. Hands wandering more as each breath intensified—bodies responding in private ways.

This is the last time I'm ever doing this, Wren said into Jamila's open mouth. Their lips parted and closed. Teeth colliding—jaws in strain. His breath smelled strongly of mint and alcohol. His taste stung her tongue. Neither of them believed what he said.

*

Wren carries Jamila into the accommodation with her legs wrapped around his waist. Through the living room. Into her room. She falls onto the bed like it is a trampoline—they both make a comment about this at the same time and laugh. Come here. This is Wren. It is said with a carnal intensity that singes every last nerve ending in Jamila's body. Her fingers are TV static. She goes. Wren is sitting with his legs crossed and Jamila is before him on her knees—tailbone to ankles. Wren rubs his hands up her back slowly, tension building with every centimeter of skin traversed. Her body collapses into his at the feeling. Ruth used to kiss my neck a lot. Okay. Jamila does it—with bite and tongue and ardor. She feels him on her teeth and knows hunger. Wren's breathing betrays him and his hands get lost in her shirt. Can I get rid of this? Yes. The T-shirt is above her head, then in his hands, then on the floor. She closes her eyes. James used to lick my armpits sometimes. Okay. Wren does this. In this moment, they both know love is a bizarre thing that fosters bizarre compulsions, and they will follow these compulsions until the day they each die. He licks her armpit again and Jamila's body tremors reactively in a way it never has before. Cologne haunts the action, and it produces the most wretched feeling Jamila has felt in all her life. So abject, so strong, she almost hates it.

Jamila pulls Wren's face into her hands in a maniacal scramble. As though if she doesn't get a hold of him, she'll die. She's after the real thing now. She's all want, dripping with desire.

He holds her. He shivers. She whines.

Ruth, he says.

James.

Ruth, he says again, eyes closed, voice cracking.

SOMETHING ABOUT US

Eden was first introduced to Connor on her twenty-fourth birthday. She posted photos of herself on Twitter that got enough traction that they ended up on his timeline. He'd messaged her immediately—something along the lines of, What's that tattoo on your forearm mean? It was a lazy first talking point, but she figured he thought it clever enough.

Eden did a double take at her phone while turning up the music, assessing the unfamiliar name on the screen with a confused smile. The tattoo in question was an assortment of abstract lines falling together to create a misshapen, scalene triangle. The ink had faded so much Eden was shocked he even acknowledged it as a tattoo and not some obscuration of light, or even a scratch.

eden: a friend of mine got bored once and stick and poked it on me. It doesn't mean anything lol I just like geometric things.

He replied again with an image of a tattoo on his thigh, just low enough that it could be partially seen in the summer, peaking beneath his shorts, but risqué enough for an initial interaction. It was one skinny rectangle between two identically sized squares: a makeshift Rothko. What do you think of this? He asked. She got the image, whispered, What the fuck, to herself under a laugh, wondering what would provoke him to do such a thing so soon. She set her drink down and zoomed in on it. The black ink raised on his pale skin, still red and irritated around the lines—an image taken freshly after it had been done.

eden: u go around just sending unsolicited thigh pics to strangers lmao
connor: if it calls for it

connor: and the moment called for it
connor: (because I knew you would like it)
eden: ahhhh but u dont know that I liked it tho, see
connor: it's geometric isn't it? happy birthday btw

Their messages contained a certain flirtatious teasing that veered on com-
bativeness. In person, these messages may be said with a cautious grin as
the space between the two slowly collapsed. Careful touches. Intentional,
playful, antagonism. After messaging back and forth, Connor asked if he
could have Eden's number, and she said: sure i guess lol. All of this online
interaction happened while at her birthday "party," which was her ten closest friends squeezed into her tiny two-bedroom Chicago apartment. The
room was perfumed with beer and wings; all the cleaned bones sitting in a
communal plate next to the TV. Eden would look down at her phone and
reply when she went to get a drink or go to the bathroom. She was taken
aback when he'd asked for her number. It was always a possibility—she
knew this—but online interaction presents a level of distance, and that
step routinely brings things back to reality.

As her friends flicked through the collaborative party playlist, Eden
found his Instagram profile. Connor Beck. Went to school in Chicago.
He was from Austin—presently living in Austin. From looking she could
see his last post was on his birthday. February 6th. Meaning, he was an
Aquarius, which never meant anything good for her. He was average
height, with slight freckles and dark brown hair that hung at his ears. She
looked deeper, saw that he'd previously had an entirely shaved head, and
decided he looked better that way—more stoic. There were only two photos of him and the rest were blurry photos of random things. Light posts,
mailboxes, a stack of books. She finished her glass of wine and turned the
phone around so the rest of the room could see the photo of him with the
shaved head. Does anyone know this guy? she asked.

Trinity and her boyfriend both looked down with drunk eyes, shook
their heads and then tripped over each other's socked feet on the smooth

apartment tile. Some of the others evaluated Connor before coming to the same conclusion. Eden went to fill up her glass with the bottle by the window and slurred, His profile says he went to DePaul. You don't know him, Ari? I think he did film there. Ari grabbed the phone from her and clicked through his profile. She leaned a flannel clad elbow against the kitchen counter and smacked her hand down at her revelation. Ah, she said. He follows Remi and Xavier. He probably was in film club with them.

Text them and ask what they think of him, she said.

Is your interest piqued? Trinity asked, taunting.

Eden laughed and put her phone in her pocket before anyone wanted to see more.

He just asked for my number.

What happened to med school guy? Ari asked.

Still there. I'm just curious.

Eden pulled out a deck of cards and asked who wanted to be her spades partner. Trinity abandoned her boyfriend for the opportunity, and all of them played spades sloppily until the night began to swallow itself into light. As everyone began to leave, Ari showed Eden the texts from the group chat with her DePaul friends:

Remi Townes: he's fine I guess
X: fine is the perfect word for it lmao
Remi Townes: ya he's nice enough
Remi Townes: crazy pretentious but like whatever
X: and very into himself

Eden thanked Ari as she stepped out of the apartment. When empty, Trinity and Eden hugged each other long and relaxed before sauntering back to their respective rooms. Trinity shouted Happy Birthday and Eden said thank you, before shutting her eyes, and sleeping till three the next day.

Eden woke up to a slew of texts from Connor, not immediately recognizing the name before the entire drunken exchange came back to her. She rubbed her eyes and let the wet goo smear onto her face.

Connor Beck: have u ever played firewatch
Connor Beck: it seems ur speed
10:14 am

Connor Beck: ok that's an assumption bc i don't know u that well
11:15 am

Connor Beck: did ur erl piercing hurt btw I kinda want one
Connor Beck: (that's a lie but like it looks super good on u)
2:19 pm

Connor Beck: damn u sleep late
3:03 pm

Trin, she said stumbling out of bed. Come look at this. Eden was in a tank top and a decaying pink pair of CVS panties. Trinity was in the living room cooking a delayed brunch of shrimp and grits. What, she said, stirring the pot—adding cayenne and red pepper flakes heavy handedly. Eden showed her the string of texts.

Goodness fuck.

It's kinda fun, though. Eden brought the phone back to her chest.

Are you gonna tell him you're seeing that guy? Trinity brought a spoon of her concoction to Eden's face. Eden blew on it but burned the roof of her mouth anyways.

She shrugged. I don't know. We're not dating.

Trinity tried the food for herself, then said, The purgatory of the talking stage. I don't miss it.

When Trinity was done Eden sat down with her food and texted Connor back. Actually yes, she had played Firewatch. What ending did she get? The protagonist and the girl never got close. Which did he get? The exact opposite. The conversation shifted into music, as it always did with guys like him. Then movies. They didn't like any of the same things. Eden unabashedly loved pop music above everything else—found merit in how sonically pleasing a beautifully crafted pop song was. Have you ever heard someone get the formula just right? She asked him once. To crack the code of something so universally enjoyable. You don't find that interesting?

No, he did not. He mentioned he had not expected her to be one of those girls—he didn't get that vibe from her. She asked him what kind of girls he meant specifically, but he didn't offer much else other than: You know what I mean. Connor also wasn't one that enjoyed playful debate or the fun tension inside of it, so they stayed away from music all together.

What Eden learned very quickly was that, yes, Connor loved to talk about himself—especially his job. He made a lot of money working in finance and would openly discuss his salary with her. She could never tell if it was to make her like him or to make himself feel big, as she was always struggling and working at a plant shop. These things, he was aware of.

I hate my job, he said on the phone about three weeks after they had begun talking. But I just got a bonus.

Good for you.

So, I can finally get that watch I've been talking about. Which one do you like more?

Connor sent Eden two photos of wrist watches—one gold, one black, both with the price glaring prominently in the corner, with no attempt at cropping it out.

Is this supposed to make me like you? And black.

He laughed. Is it working?

Eden would lay in bed and text him back. Talk to him while on her runs. While doing her make-up. The more time that passed it became clear to her that she did not like him, but for some reason she couldn't stop talking to him. He was arrogant and the least self-aware person she'd ever met, but there were moments where he would say just the right thing in the most vulnerable way, and all she could do was succumb to her humanity.

Eden was seeing a med student named Alec at the same time. They'd met randomly while at a bar. Alec kept sending drinks her way until she gave him her number, making for five drinks in total. Alec was extremely nonchalant, and after that initial interaction, she wasn't sure how much he liked her. They'd been going on dates on and off for about a month. The most he said to her was that he thought her locs looked good, and no matter what pair she was wearing, he always said he liked her shoes.

One day she wore a pair of Converse she'd hung onto since her senior year of high school—the white rubber eroding more and more with each step she took. She and Alec were walking through downtown, hands awkwardly dangling near each other, narrowly touching. He looked down, and in a monotone voice said, I like your shoes.

I have had these since I was seventeen, she said. They're literally disgusting.

Oh, he said. Well, I like them.

They got crepes from a place on North Broadway—her, sweet Nutella and banana. Him, savory salmon and spinach. She texted Connor a picture of her shoes and said:

Eden: do u like these
Connor: of course not
Eden: exactly thank you

Who's that? Alec asked, mouth entirely full. The pinky salmon mushed into a soft pastel green, contaminated by the spinach. She saw the mound roll around on his tongue like a pin ball. There could be no redemption after that.

Eden put her phone away and took a mouthful of her crepe—mouth sticking shut with Nutella and bananas alike.

Are you attracted to me? she asked.

Alec stopped drinking his water mid swig and set it down.

Of course. Why would you ask me that?

It just doesn't seem like it, she said.

Sorry. I'm not good with my words, I guess.

The rest of the date was a formality. The sun beat down on them, as if it had a vendetta and wanted to make everything as unbearable as possible. Sweat poured into every crevice of exposed skin, making any physical contact intolerable. Alec made a few stale jokes about the heat, then his mom and how much he hated her, which felt like a red flag. Then, he walked her home, and just as he went in for a kiss, she turned her cheek towards him. Alec kind of chuckled to himself with a hand behind his neck and said, Alright then.

When she got inside, she sent Connor a photo of herself, and he said back: You look good as fuck.

After a day or two, she informed Alec things wouldn't work out.

Eden and Connor continued like this—texting, flirting. Eden never with any intention of meeting or dating him. Connor with every intention of that, despite how wrong Eden thought they clearly were for each other. Things ended so organically and suddenly with Alec she never had to confront Connor and tell him she was seeing someone, which was something she was worried about. She enjoyed having someone to talk to. He was extremely direct—one of the only things she actually liked about him. He told her daily how attractive she was—and sometimes when drunk, what he'd like to do to her—with her—if they were in the same place. It was said with such assurance, devoid of trepidation, that whenever it happened it was always more intriguing than off-putting. Even if misplaced, his blind confidence was amusing, just enough to keep her around.

Connor was equally brash when it came to the other side of things. Five months after her birthday, Eden decided to shave her head. She was tired of having locs and wanted to do away with hair all together.

I'm cutting my hair off today, she said to him on the phone, running into a beauty store.

Should you, though? Through the phone was the distinct sound of him cooking dinner, stainless steel scraping stainless steel.

It'll look good, she said, defensive.

If you say so.

That night after dinner, Trinity took the clippers to Eden's head, and after she watched the once pieces of her hair hit the ground, she excitedly ran to the bathroom mirror and admired herself. The sharpness of her face was more prominent now, and for a moment she felt like she owned her beauty. This high was quickly disrupted by Connor, and his simple response to the cut: if you're happy.

I hate him. I don't know why I put up with him, she said to Trinity. She was tidying the living room and folding up blankets. Busy work, really, to distract herself.

Then be done with him. Trinity was half listening, looking at her phone. This was a conversation they had had many times before. Eden's aversion to Connor. Trinity's attempt to guide her in the right direction. Eden never listening. Trinity looked up from her phone and began to walk into her room, saying, Be done with him or stop talking about it.

Eden did try this time, more than before. She didn't reply to him for three months. She knew it wouldn't affect him, though. Connor was shameless. A sequence of unanswered texts was not a deterrent to him. If anything, it was ammunition or a challenge. It didn't matter—he always kept coming back.

It was beneficial—cozy even—that Connor lived in Texas. She didn't have to worry about running into him or justifying herself. So, she started dating again. A guy from work, whom she was impartial toward, but who loved buying her things. For him, working at the plant shop was just for fun—he didn't need it. This was very casual, and they saw each other, at most, twice a week. But after three months, they both decided it wasn't going anywhere and called it a day.

Eden hypothesized Connor had a sixth sense for when things were going wrong for her—that's when she was most valuable to him, she figured.

A week after that breakup Connor sent her a YouTube video on how to make rosemary focaccia, something they'd talked about liking before. Have you ever made this? He asked.

Only ate, she said. Never made.

Let's both make it tonight.

They spent that night on the phone, cooking together. She didn't remember why she stopped talking to him in the first place. It felt far off at that point. It was January—things were anew. She watched Connor's small hands mold and dimple the dough in the tiny phone screen next to the stove. She repeated the same steps and allowed herself, for a second, to enjoy this moment as a singular positive thing. She would deal with the rest later.

For a while, cooking on the phone became routine. Trinity would be sure to stay in her room or be out of the house at these times. Eden was embarrassed on some level, and on another, it was just enough to get by. They went through tikka masala, fried catfish, sweet and spicy salmon, and a nice short rib winter stew. Trinity would always come home and taste-test it through somewhat gritted teeth. Though, when it came to the short rib, she cracked a smile and said, Yeah. That's fucking good.

This went on for a month.

One night, while drunkenly talking on the phone, Connor told Eden that he felt generally unfulfilled in life.

It's just, he began, I'm twenty-seven and I already feel bored.

I get it, she sighed. Eden was painting her raw, bitten nails neon green. She wasn't doing a good job.

I'm sure everyone feels this way, and it isn't unique in the slightest, but I feel very bored and sad most days. Connor sighed and then said, You're the first person I've admitted that to.

I'm a good person to tell secrets to.

You think? She heard the crinkling sound of him repositioning himself on the bed.

You haven't thought about that? The distance.

I guess you're right. We're so far removed. We present no consequences to each other.

Eden nodded. A relationship of convenience of sorts. I'm just, like, your void to talk into without repercussion.

My little void, he laughed.

Yep. And you're mine.

You're right, it is convenient. Although, he began. He let it hang for entirely too long.

Although, she lead, tensing up.

I do want to come to Chicago sometime.

Sure, she said half-heartedly. What would you do if you came here? What friends would you stay with?

Connor laughed, somewhat defeated, and Eden heard the distinct sound of a pint hitting a wooden table. Yeah, I don't know, he said. I thought I did, but maybe I should re-evaluate.

The conversation dissolved thereafter, and Eden hung up under the pretense of needing to shower. She talked to Trinity about Connor—I can't believe he actually thinks he is coming here—but Trinity had checked out, chopping onions for her shakshuka in the morning.

I wish you would just date someone you like.

I'm not dating him.

I wish you would talk to someone you like. Or someone that likes you, even. Like, as a person.

I can go ghost again. If that's what you want, Eden said.

I stopped caring last year. She pushed the onion bits off the large knife and placed them in the tomato concoction. Do what you want.

Eden did. She returned to dating apps—something she generally detested but it felt inevitable. A guy named Costas "super liked" her, which was so bold she felt she had to give him a chance. Their first date was a simple one—they got ice cream. At the very end, in the silence that lingered, he said very seriously: I'd really like to take care of you.

In what way? Eden laughed. The heat of his knee across from hers was a furnace. Then, the slow pressure of that contact, making it more intentional, sensual.

This ended in Eden on her back in bed, then Costas, then them pressed skin to skin, rolling around. It was glorious—they lay in bed, sweat doused, panting, saying through laughter, How was that so good? It set a precedent. Every single time they saw each other they had sex. In bathrooms, in shopping mall dressing rooms, in the kitchen, in cars. Once, in his backyard around a campfire, and the tickling feeling of the grass on her bare back kept her laughing the whole time, so they didn't get much done. This was them. Their relationship became so intrinsically intwined with the sex she wondered if that's all it was. When she would speak to him, he didn't usually have much to say back, and waited for her to finish talking so they could get to it. When they did talk it was very flat, lacking any real substance or emotional connection. It simply was easier to fuck. He was never pushy or mean—she believed he genuinely liked her, in his own limited way. She just figured he wasn't able to understand desire and romantic interest as separate things.

The first month of this was exciting and decadent. She would tell stories to Trinity and Ari at brunch and they would say how jealous they were—how thrilling and animalistic everything seemed. Trinity seemed happy, which made Eden happy—See, she said, isn't this better than Connor?—but she knew she couldn't keep up the ruse. Each week that passed she confronted the urge to end it all.

Eden forgot about this particular incident for a while, but two weeks after Eden and Costas's first date he said he could see himself marrying her.

Oh, Eden said.

What? You don't think so? He smiled and washed the dishes.

I mean. I don't really know you so much yet.

Right. But you can usually tell those things, can't you?

I suppose.

Before Eden could ask how he could be so sure of that when he hardly knew anything about her, he picked her up and set her on the kitchen counter—stealing a kiss instead of asking for one, which was the sort of thing she liked. She had not thought of this moment again until the day before her 25th birthday when she broke up with him. His face turned puppy-like, asking why, telling her that he loved her.

That's not possible, she said. We hardly talk about anything.

That's not true.

What's my middle name?

They were sitting on a bench outside her apartment, directly across the street from a McDonald's. Costas was beautiful, which made this break-up exceptionally hard. They sat in silence for ten whole minutes. In the eleventh minute, she saw Costas do a small nod in the soft light of the lamp post above them. He kissed her on the cheek and walked away in the wrong direction of his train.

Once out of sight, Eden called Connor and asked about his day.

For her 25th birthday, Eden previously had reservations with Costas at a sushi omakase restaurant. Trinity filled in instead.

Once there, Trinity asked what happened with Costas. The restaurant was dim lit—somewhat blue-black, swallowing their frames. Trinity's shoulders in her black jacket bled into the darkness around her, and the bold soft light above them felt like spotlights. They picked up the nigiri with their fingers—soft and malleable in their hands—and looked at each other for a face of confirmation. Trinity's eyebrows went up. Good? Eden nodded and let it all melt into her mouth

So, what—you didn't like him? Trinity asked.

It wasn't a matter of that. We just had no real connection. She sipped her sake.

You run through 'em Eden, I swear.

Not on purpose. I just haven't found anything that feels real.

Eden felt a warmth pool in her chest and looked onward, waiting for the next round of food to be brought out. The restaurant only had eight seats—barstools sitting next to each other, and she felt embarrassed at the prospect of them listening in on her romantic failings.

She sat in between Trinity and a man that came alone. The last four members of their breakfast club were a group of old college friends who kept the conversation going on their end of the bar, which left the lone guy in the middle sandwiched between two groups of people that were only speaking to each other.

Before Trinity could bring up anything else, marinated bluefin tuna was brought to them on a small bed of rice.

After eating it, the man to Eden's right said, to no one in particular, I could take another ten of those.

Eden turned to him, only slightly. I know, she said soft, in case she was intruding. You think we can get some to go?

I'll ask if you ask, he joked. Lead the way.

Eden and Trinity spent the rest of the night talking to the guy. His name was Kofi. The undertones of his brown skin grew warmer as the night went on and the sake made home in their bodies, loosening up gears. A few courses in, he and Trinity bonded over a shared guilty pleasure documentary on Netflix about horses.

You won't watch it with her? He teased.

Eden isn't really an animal person.

Eden . . . he tsked.

It's true. Horses kind of scare me.

She heard of someone getting collapsed ribs from being kicked in the chest, Trinity said, just as the next course was brought to them. She hasn't recovered since.

I wouldn't have thought, Kofi said with a hand on the back of her chair. You seem to have a very calming aura. Very snow-white-esque.

My God, Trinity laughed. Now, *that* is hysterical.

I really am no good around animals. I could never live on a farm.

Kofi laughed to himself just as Eden and Trinity did. You're easy to talk to, though. Maybe my bias is showing.

Kofi's eyes met Eden's before continuing in conversation with Trinity. Eden turned her head to the left, to hide how affected she was.

The next dish was a king salmon topped with roe. Eden ate hers before both Kofi or Trinity and made a noise of satisfaction so loud it elicited a humored response from the entire bar, the chef included.

I feel bad. Now I feel like I should give you mine, Kofi said.

I won't say no. It is my birthday, after all.

This is true—this is very true. He picked it up with his fingers, cupped hand under her chin—rings cold kissing her jaw—and fed it to her. They maintained eye contact as she took the one bite and attempted to chew through the smile that threatened her mouth.

Satisfied?

She nodded her head and attempted to ignore Trinity whispering encouragement in her ear.

Yes, she said. Thank you.

The three of them spent the rest of the night talking to each other—Eden and Kofi playfully going back and forth—matching each other in wits until the bills came and it was time to go. He started walking with Eden and Trinity back to the Red Line. He sat between them, his body with a natural lean towards Eden. Eden's hand thought hard about whether it should land on his knee. But they'd all got lost in conversation and Kofi's stop snuck up on them quicker than they'd expected. He'd gotten up, rushed, nearly sandwiched between the double doors. He said, It was really nice meeting you guys, and something else that got lost as the train doors closed.

You didn't get his number, Trinity said, closing the space he'd previously filled.

I know. I thought he'd get mine.

You can find him, she said, on the internet, probably.

Maybe. He seemed very "offline," Eden said in air quotes. So maybe that was just it.

No one is really offline, are they?

Some of the best people are.

You're online, Trinity laughed.

Who says I'm so great? Eden nudged Trinity in the side and laid her head on her shoulder. This may be strange to say, she began again. But that was the most I'd felt in a long time.

What do you mean?

Like, Eden closed her eyes. I don't know. When you feel jittery and hopeful. Like an instant crush. It just hits you, and you feel stupid. Do you know what I mean?

Sure, she laughed. I guess.

Did you feel that way with Jared?

Trinity looked forward for a moment then shook her head. No, she said. Very close, but no. It wasn't an instantaneous feeling. I did like him—I do like him. But I think after a while of him asking me out I was just like, why not?

Eden pressed her cheek hard into Trinity's shoulder and wrapped her hands around her arm. She almost asked if she regretted it, but figured she already knew the answer.

Eden woke in the middle of the night, still high from the excitement of dinner, and searched the name Kofi into every single social media app—LinkedIn included. But none of them were him, and half of them didn't have profile pictures. With the final search her hope died.

Instead, she texted Connor a photo of her meal that night. He responded immediately, despite the fact that it was two in the morning, saying happy birthday and that he was jealous.

Around this time was maybe the most she and Connor consistently spoke. She really indulged in the conversations—got her money's worth, wrung every good thing out of the interaction. He would sometimes make sly comments about the books she read or the music she listened too, but she didn't care. It was an accepted consequence of their bond. Sometimes she wondered what he was doing on the other side of things—if he was actively dating, too. He never really mentioned it, and she didn't either. One night, a month and a half after her birthday, on a call, he said that his girlfriend had dumped him.

I didn't know you had a girlfriend, she said.

Yeah. For about eight months.

Did she know about me?

She found out, he said. We got into a fight about it a while ago. I told her you were just a friend, which you are, technically.

Right. She was washing the dishes while talking to him with her headphones in. I can never tell what this is to you, she said. Like, are you actually into me?

Of course, he said. The only reason nothing is happening is because of you.

Right.

Are you into me?

Truthfully, she said. I don't know. Sometimes you can be very charming, other times you can be an asshole.

Fair.

The conversation diverted into an anime he was watching and had recently gotten her into. While talking about the third episode, Eden interrupted by saying, I don't think we're very good for each other.

You think, he said sarcastically. But I like having you around. It's like, home base.

That's a good way of putting it.

And, at the risk of you completing ignoring me for months on end again, I still really want to meet you.

Eden watched the dishes swim around in the soapy pool of the sink.

What are you doing three weekends from now?

Connor had decided to come to Chicago. A compromise—he would get a hotel room in case Eden changed her mind. He didn't want to end up homeless because she decided to disappear again. He was ecstatic, asking her what things they should do. Should they go to the MCA? See a movie? There was an Asian bakery in Chinatown that sold these pork buns she was always raving about, and he wanted to put a taste with a name. I feel like I'm stepping into the TV show that is your life, he said. Things are about to become tactile.

The Friday he arrived they decided to meet at a French bakery in Logan Square after he settled into his place. It was his favorite when he was going to school there. Eden headed to the Red Line. Her hair was grown out then, somewhat low-cut and curly. Close to her head and dyed blond. Connor eagerly texted her and she responded, more indifferent than it probably came off in text. She sat on the train, preparing to get off and transfer to the Blue Line. She was listening to Daft Punk's *Discovery.* When track nine came on she wondered how long this would go on. If a year from now they would continue to default to each other until right place right time occurred, if ever. And if it didn't? Another year would pass. Would she be thirty ignoring him for a month, then flying to Texas to see him, getting coffee that was just good enough but not amazing, enduring slights in the hopes that it would be followed by a compliment at just the right frequency, on just a bad enough day?

She thought about how the trains were smoother in Chicago than they were in New York, watching things pass by the window and blur into a beautiful, ineffable something. Something abstract and gooey where reality and desire spoke to each other with more than just want. Infront of this blur, sitting across from her, was a man who was already looking at her. Dark hair and a bagel in a ring clad hand. Perhaps the blonde hair threw him off, but when Eden returned the gaze, as amazed and piercing as his, he leaned back and crossed one leg over the other.

You, Kofi said, grinning.

Me, Eden said, in a stunned whisper.

Sorry I ran out like that last time, he said. Someone was distracting me, and I almost missed my stop.

Eden laughed. How dare they?

It's alright. I enjoyed it.

He kicked his foot out and touched her shoe in the open aisle of the train car. She caught a girl watching them out of the corner of her eye.

What are you up to? She asked him, low under her breath.

He shrugged his shoulders casually and the leather of his jacket made a soft noise. Kofi smiled at her. I don't know, he said.

When the stop for her to transfer to the Blue Line came, she didn't get off. They kept talking. They rode to the end of the line, and both realized in the same instant that somewhere along the way they'd sacrificed their days to keep talking to each other.

This is funny, he said, as they got off at the very last stop.

It is.

Do you not have anywhere to be?

Eden turned off her phone and shook her head. No, she said. Not really.

They traversed up the subway steps, through the turnstiles, and out into the air. It was summer and everyone was there, confronting the heat body-first. In front of them, two women walked with a baby in a stroller. In the distance, a college-age boy took a headphone out to speak to the woman sitting on the bench. In a coffee shop window, a woman reached her hand across the table to the person on the other side. When their palms met, they were both shaking.

ALONE
IN THE
MIDDLE OF
THE WORLD

Late March, Ciara's co-worker—Angelina—asked if she would help house-sit her apartment. The two women were at a hole-in-the-wall diner five minutes from their job.

I'm going on a trip, she said without eye contact, stirring her coffee with the tail-end of her fork. I just need you to feed my dog and get the mail for me. Can you do that?

Ciara sipped her drink and agreed. She didn't think much of it. A few insomniac nights before she'd watched *Yes Man* and under the blissful, transformative post theater spell, figured her life too could be positively altered by obliging to things. Angelina told Ciara she would take Monday, Wednesday, and Friday, and her boyfriend Elias would take the remaining days.

Angelina had unsettling green eyes and usually well-kept brown hair that had become stringy, and grease-filled, like limp grass. She smelled of perspiration and wet copper, and the rigorous bounce of her left leg shook the table. Ciara brought her nose to her coffee and quietly inhaled.

When Angelina asked Ciara to get food after work, Ciara initially thought Angelina was in danger. They hardly knew each other. When they sat down to eat, Angelina simply asked how Ciara was—asked about the shape of her personal life. What did she do outside of work? It was clear something was coming. The preamble leading up to her proposition was excruciatingly polite. There were long pauses where she gave Ciara the room to expand on her life but there was nothing to offer. She considered making something up—a vibrant, alluring morsel of information—but instead told Angelina about the on and off mouse infestation in her building and how, by her luck, it hadn't reached her unit yet.

That is very lucky, Angelina said, affectless.

They've given us complimentary traps, too.

The girls had only been working together for a few months—book-sellers at a store nearby. Only occasionally working the same shift. When they did, they would strike up an easy conversation about an author or a customer that would reach its inevitable demise not even three minutes later. They agreed on Baldwin and disagreed on Hemmingway. Their relationship was entirely contextual, as Ciara found many adult relationships to be.

After Ciara agreed to help, Angelina thanked her by sliding a White Barn candle across the table in an all-blue dollar store gift bag.

When will you be back? Ciara asked.

Angelina bit into a soggy piece of French toast and said, diplomatically, I'm not sure of the timeline yet. She then pointed to the gift bag and told Ciara that inside were keys, and a piece of paper with directions for her dog, apartment, and general upkeep.

I should say, I've never had a pet before. I don't know how much you'd want to trust me with your dog's well-being. Can't you take him with you?

Angelina shook her head.

It's for the best, she said. I'm in no place to take care of a living being at the moment.

It was so alarmingly blunt, Ciara couldn't think of a thing to say.

Outside, in the parking lot, Angelina was a dark silhouette on the sky's blazing background.

She told Ciara she would send money routinely for her help.

Do you need my information? Ciara asked.

That won't be necessary.

The woman looked at Ciara as though the following words were an arduous chore. Then in a low breath she said, I'm sorry for the burden.

Angelina was next to the driver's side then, wearing a white T-shirt and oversized blue jeans that swallowed her small legs wide like a double-barreled shotgun. Then, she got in and sped away—car disappearing into the cadmium of the horizon.

*

Angelina left town the first day of April—the same day Ciara's high school best friend Jordan came to visit. She was passing through while driving to the neighboring state. Jordan had called two nights before with a voice like a startled child. When Ciara picked up, she was doom scrolling on the internet, waiting for her melatonin to kick in. A bill had been passed to make abortion difficult in her state. A rapper was shot. Amazon had 15% off select electronics for the next twenty-four hours—all presented in that order.

I have to drive to a conference in a few days, Jordan said through the static of the phone. Can I see you? Please?

The girls got drinks at a place downtown that had succulents as center pieces and Edison lights hanging down like ropes. The bartenders had beards and blue eyes, and there was no menu aside from a QR code on a napkin by the water dispenser. Ciara had gotten into the habit of taking stock of everything she saw. It helped her remain in her own body.

A half empty bottle of Jose Cuervo. A girl's cuffed white Forces. A plaque on the wall, commemorating the low-income housing project the bar had previously been.

Ciara watched as Jordan ordered them both Kentucky mules. Jordan had filled out; grown a woman's hips and somehow a child's round race. Ciara had only ever known her as a thin bone.

I didn't even think, Jordan said handing Ciara the mule. You don't like bourbon, do you?

I do now, actually. Ciara took a sip of the drink.

Since when?

Since living here.

The girls talked about life with the outline social media provided. How was the trip to Rome? Jordan would never go back. How was Ciara's mother? In Germany—touring as a backup singer. Jordan said she and her fiancé just got a house but that their biannual hiking trips out west fizzled the past two years. As is life, she said quietly.

Jordan wanted to know how Ciara's painting class was, and Ciara admitted to quitting a while ago. So much money, not much pay off. It was more of a group outing she'd come to notice.

I have to say, Jordan began, with a certain caution. I had the opportunity to fly to my conference—all expenses paid—but I felt this strong urge to see you.

Ciara sat back. Really?

Jordan nodded. Arman and I were going through old Facebook album's the other night, and I saw the pictures of all of us in LA for your twenty-first. He pointed to you and said, who's that? She took a sip and the strength of the drink forced her to bare her teeth. I asked if he was joking and he said no. I talk about you all the time, but he's never seen a photo of you. Isn't that strange?

Oh, I don't know. Ciara tinkered with her bracelet.

You know that it is. It really troubled me. I mean you're my oldest friend and we haven't seen each other in four years. I started thinking about everyone else too; then my home and my job, and then I felt I didn't have a grasp on anything going on. Jordan paused for a moment and chewed on the inside of her cheek. I live in New England of all places. Arman adores his job, and I love him, but I drive an hour away to get my hair done. The only people I see are university spouses, and they know nothing about me. On my birthday last year, I took a walk and had breakfast in bed, then fell asleep at nine. Like, God—I'm only twenty-eight. She looked away from Ciara and played with the engagement ring on her finger. I think the circumstances of life changed so quickly. By the time the new normal had set in, there was nothing left for me to do about it.

How do you mean?

Jordan averted her eyes. I feel far away from everything in my life.

There was the tired slouch of her shoulders. Her collarbones pierced through the taunt skin of her chest.

I didn't tell you, Ciara began. But I was laid off a few months ago.

From the marketing job? Ciara nodded her head. Oh, God. I'm so sorry.

She told her it was alright. It was a cost cutting decision.

Jordan got them two more mules and took the seat next to her when she returned. Ciara leaned her head on Jordan's shoulder and the hairs on the side of her afro tickled the inside of Ciara's ear.

Did you ever go camping with those people? The ones from your old job? You were talking about it, I remember.

Ciara shook her head. We all talked for a while after I was laid off. But you know how those things go. Ciara picked up her drink.

Jordan put her hand on Ciara's leg.

I don't like to think about you out here all on your own.

I'm not all on my own, Ciara lied.

Jordan played with a napkin and took a long drink. In middle school, she began, I remember thinking that I always made my best friends right before summer. And, as you know, my parents didn't let me have a phone until I was sixteen, so I lost all the progress I'd made by the time we were back in school. Most of the kids in my neighborhood were much older than me—which was fine. I felt an ego inflating pride when accepted by them. But I felt such a loss of real connection in between those months. I had a babysitter named Madison that would watch me during the summers. And for reasons I won't get into she caused a lot of tension in the house, so eventually I lost her.

Your father, I'm assuming.

You've met him. You know. Jordan gave an apologetic smile. After that, I'd watch the same DVD's over and over. Wrote plays for my stuffed animals. Read on the porch outside. It sounds liberating but it became joylessly monotonous faster than you'd think.

Ciara couldn't see Jordan's face. There was only the red brick wall across from her and the haunting portrait of Jim Morrison staring back at her, surrounded by the stark faces of other white musicians on their own posters.

There's something uniquely tortuous about being sad and alone in the summer. So sticky and suffocating, Jordan said. Like it's climbing all over you.

They talked until the sky dimmed the natural light of the bar, then Ciara told Jordan about her commitment, and said she had to go. They walked through downtown—past collages of college students pressed into herds—into the parking garage where their cars resided. Jordan hugged Ciara before getting in—clasping both hands together behind her back for a firm grip.

I'll call you next Thursday. Jordan squeezed her hand and Ciara nodded her head—searing the memory of the heat into her cold palm like a brand.

*

Angelina's apartment had been gutted.

A mostly empty bookshelf. A stripped bed. A TV stand, outlined with dust from where the television had once lived. The dog cowered in the corner at the sight of Ciara, rubbing its eyes into the carpet, then hiding behind the long plastic blinds.

everythings gone, she texted Jordan

Jordan replied, whats that white girl gotten you into??

She collected Angelina's mail, stuffed it in a drawer. Took the dog on a walk, refilled the food and water, and then went back home.

Ciara's weekend was dedicated to attempting to find Angelina online. She managed to have no digital footprint. The only thing that turned up was an old newspaper article from the *Charleston Gazette* about a speech competition she won as a middle schooler. She stood in front of a mansion of a house—with Roman columns and an expansive veranda on the second floor. The camera flash bounced off the reflective trophy. In the photo,

Angelina had blinked.

Once finished, Ciara turned on a show and attempted to sing along to the theme song. Her voice cracked into something unforgiveable. She hadn't spoken out loud all day.

That Monday, when she returned to the apartment, Angelina had mailed Ciara an envelope with her name on it. Forty dollars were inside with a note that said: more two weeks from now. There was no return address.

Two weeks later, another envelope in her name arrived, and again two weeks after that.

There was an eerie air to the correspondence. How detached and vague it was, but she couldn't find it in herself to stop going to the apartment. The money was consistent and timely. Above all, she needed it. Angelina upheld her end of the bargain; though there was a level of deception, she hadn't been entirely lied to.

After the first two weeks, the dog took to Ciara—running to her feet when she opened the front door. Jumping up when she grabbed his leash or opened the cabinet where his food was stored. By then she figured the dog had come to understand her as a mysterious, recurrent deity whose purpose was to keep his life in motion. The week after that she thought maybe the dog loved her.

All of April, Ciara and Jordan consistently spoke on Thursdays. Jordan began going to the gym, thinking it would foster a sense of community.

The trouble is there's a sort of unspoken code in these environments. Not everyone wants to be spoken to, Jordan said. Ciara could hear her cooking in the background. There's a dark-skinned girl I see every Tuesday at noon—walking out of her group workout session as I'm walking into mine. We always nod at each other, but it's like, do I intrude?

I feel like most people in their twenties wouldn't mind being intruded upon.

Girl, Jordan chided. Come on.

I wouldn't mind. Ciara took stock of her room. A water bottle. Flonase. An empty tissue box.

Jordan had a few ideas on how to strike up a friendship, though she was still workshopping them. Ciara was lying in bed, scrolling through videos on her phone. Ever since Angelina left, dog videos were targeted to her. Dogs that looked strikingly similar to Angelina's dog. She watched one chase its tail in the middle of the street, then realized she didn't know the dog's name.

She didn't tell you? Jordan asked.

No. And I have no way to ask.

You don't have her phone number?

We hardly know each other. I thought she'd be back in like, a week or something.

I don't understand why she left him in the first place, Jordan said.

She said she couldn't take care of him.

There was a silence on the phone only filled by the hollow baritone of pans hit with wooden spoons. A television sang in the background.

I don't know if that girl is coming back, Jordan said.

Ciara thought about it before—on and off over the weeks. She considered it then, and after another few weeks passed, subconsciously knew it to be true. Early June, there was a piece of paper sitting on Angelina's kitchen counter that said: This is Angelina's ex-boyfriend. If you haven't given up yet, give me a call if you'd like.

*

Elias was tall and thin; light brown locs that stopped at his ears and thick rimmed black prescription glasses that magnified his brown eyes insect-like. In the open space under the booth his legs stretched all the way to the other side. He and Ciara were sitting at a family-owned barbecue spot hidden in the quiet part of downtown.

Elias told her he had cycled through all the stages of grief; only a day or two ago finding solace in acceptance.

I was angry for a while, and then I was just sad. We weren't in love ever, but she was my best and only friend here. Hey—thanks man.

The waiter set waters down in front of them and they both ordered. Ciara watched Elias talk to the waiter—it seemed he'd waited on him before. Elias led the conversation, asking how he was. It was clear the waiter enjoyed talking to him but had things to do. It gave the interaction an uneasiness to it, but Elias charged through the discomfort headfirst.

Ciara found it odd to imagine Elias and Angelina together. There was a candidness to him. Not in an abrasive, off putting way, but as though he had nothing to hide, and let everything come tumbling out of him no matter the audience. They seemed to be opposites. Perhaps that's why it worked. Him—self-assured, leading. Her—quiet, closing in on herself.

Elias told her he'd been worried initially but had come to many of the same conclusions as Ciara had over the weeks. Toward the middle of May he went into the bookstore and asked one of their managers if he knew why Angelina hadn't been showing up to work. He told him she'd put in her two weeks back in March.

I know that you guys were good friends, he said. I'm sorry you have to go through this, too.

Oh. Ciara put her straw in her glass. We weren't really. I mean, we were hardly acquaintances.

When I asked her about work, Angelina told me you two were close. You and some other girls named May and Alexis.

Well, we would talk occasionally—all of us—but we had never crossed that line. We'd never become friends. When she asked me to look after her place, I assumed she had no one else to ask.

Elias raised both eyebrows. Could be part of it.

He vetted himself—showed her pictures of them together ranging from January to two weeks before she left. Them at dinner. Them walking the track of the local high school, bundled up during the winter. Them playing video games at the Barcade downtown. Even in these photos they didn't appear as two people that knew each other intimately. They seemed haphazardly stitched together.

She'd broken up with him undramatically before she left. We are more friends than anything, she had said, and he agreed with the sentiment. He'd known this all along. Elias had moved to town eight months before for a new job. He'd met Angelina when they'd both gone to the theater alone and ended up next to each other in the very first row. Angelina had been living in town for a few weeks at that point, and they didn't waste much time before dating. They were together the following Tuesday.

What else had she told you about me? Ciara asked. About us being friends?

Small things. Your favorite essay is "Notes of a Native Son." You have all these earrings up and down your ear and were best with the harsh customers. You guys ate lunch together when you worked the same shift.

All of that was true, except the last statement. Though, for some reason, Ciara found herself nodding in validation of it all.

After dinner they took the dog for a walk in the park behind Angelina's apartment. They filled in the gaps of Angelina then the gaps of each other. Both Midwestern born. Both born in the same late nineties year. Ciara wasn't sure what to reveal, what to keep to herself.

Elias told Ciara she could stop watching the dog and the house if she wanted, but she didn't mind. To stop felt like a terrible omen. A death of sorts. A death of what, exactly? Elias wanted to know. But she couldn't put it into words. To give it a name was to attach the self to it.

Do you think she'll come back? He asked.

For some reason I hope she will. Or at least, I believe she thinks she may be back. I don't think she would leave us with this if she felt there was no possibility for return. Ciara held the leash and Elias walked beside her.

I've rebuilt my life so many times over the last few years, he said. I can't imagine choosing to do it all over again.

As they looped the track, Ciara watched a child pulled forward by the strength of a black lab, her mother following behind with outstretched arms. Three girls under a tree doing watercolor into their notebooks. A boy with his head in the lap of a woman. She stroked his hair softly— like something precious and scarce. His body folded inward, slow, like a Venus flytrap.

*

On Thursday Jordan told Ciara she'd talked to the girl at the gym.

I asked her where she got her hair done, she said. I can't believe I hadn't used that line sooner.

They'd only talked briefly, though a day later ran into each other again during an evening workout and exchanged numbers. They decided to go to a spin class together, both having been too afraid to go alone.

Towards the end of Ciara and Jordan's conversation, Ciara told Jordan about meeting up with Elias.

I don't understand. How's she paying you both?

Elias says her family is wealthy. Maybe they're helping her.

Are you sure you're alright with all this?

I'm fine. Really.

Ciara looked down at the black pants on the floor of her room, covered in miniscule dog hairs. On her bedside table: an open envelope. A twenty-dollar bill. A restaurant receipt.

The next time they spoke on the phone Jordan added a couple of their old high school friends to the call. Jordan updated them on the saga of Ciara's life in real time.

Wait, one of the girls said. Tell us from the beginning.

They all set their phones down on countertops and ordered wings from the same franchise. They took turns divulging details about their lives, and when Ciara spoke of Angelina, they girls erupted with something akin to amusement, but kinder.

Again next week? the girls asked at the end—and they all returned. The week after only two showed up and the following week it was back to just Jordan and Ciara. They spoke for only a few minutes. Ciara talked about an incident at work—they were hosting a reading, and no one turned up.

God. That sounds awful. Jordan was getting dressed and her voice sounded far away on the speaker phone. Not one person?

No, she said. But all the staff enjoyed the reading. She had a presence about her.

The girl from Jordan's gym was coming over for dinner so they had to cut the call short.

I can't believe that, Jordan sighed. Doesn't she have any friends?

Early July, Ciara got a call from Elias. She was in bed attempting to do a word search in a book she got from her job. Summer was in full swing then, which meant nothing was comfortable. In her apartment, her un-washed sweat-soaked clothes festered beneath the window, exhaling a stale musk. As she gripped her pen, sweat dripped onto the paper, making any page she touched thin and chalky.

There were times in the past—when she felt the same all-consuming weight she felt that summer—where she had intrusive thoughts about something bad happening to her. That she'd die in a car crash or be beat up and robbed. In the past, it made her feel better. In those times, she imagined friends would stay the night with her to keep her company—put her mind at ease. Pour their hearts into a black microphone in a hysteric eulogy, or that someone, once reminded of the friable nature of life, would profess their undying love to her.

She didn't have these thoughts anymore. If she had disappeared, she wasn't certain anyone would notice. She didn't have much to rob.

Elias's voice on the phone was exasperated and desperate. All his words vanished into his breath.

Would you mind coming to get me? he asked. You're the only person I know in town.

His car had run out of gas. He'd felt it happening and pulled into the park by the side of the road where a little league tournament was taking place. A white lady at the park said if he called the police, they'd help him get gas.

And I sure as hell wasn't gonna do that, he said.

Ciara said, I wouldn't want you to.

When she arrived at the park, she found him taking solace beneath the largest, most leafy tree. It was the hottest day of the summer.

I have water for you. She handed him her bottle.

He thanked her and she sat beside him as he drank. His gray shirt had turned black with perspiration, and she cleaned his glasses for him with the bottom of her shirt. His hand found her back in a thank you.

Were you busy? he asked.

She handed his glasses back, careful. Not at all.

They watched the baseball game closest to them as he finished off her water. When number twelve got up to the plate Elias said to look out for him, because he's the star. He was right. The kid hit a line drive between first and second, forcing the centerfielder to chase it to the fence. The next time he was up, he hit a fly ball into left field that the outfielder called but didn't catch. They began placing bets after that—on what he would do—and then the sky was dim, and the game was over in the fifth inning. It was a mercy rule.

They got gas and filled up his car. Then, Elias suggested ice cream. They ate it as they walked the bike path in the park.

Elias worked at a call center and told stories of the most vitriolic callers. One woman hated him because he sounded exactly like her ex-husband, and another threw slurs at him because she could "hear the black in his voice." But there were the people who were kind—which meant they asked, *how are you,* before launching into their needs. Those were his favorite people.

Ciara told him the same story she told Jordan about the writer who had the event and Elias said he would've gone, had he known.

The blue summer light fell upon them as they abandoned the trail and began heading back to the car.

Thank you, Elias said, with a gentle hand on her left shoulder. I owe you one.

His skin was darker than it was the last time she saw him, and she thought it was beautiful the way the summer had its way with him. He had been ravaged—he glowed.

At home in the shower, she turned the water ice cold and let it drill into her shoulders until her skin was numb and nerveless.

A week and a half later, Ciara found a mouse in one of her shoes.

She had been on her way to work on a Saturday and slipped a foot into one of her loafers, only to be met with a fleshy, furry presence. The miniscule black eyes of the rodent looked up at her, innocent and pleading.

She called Elias on the phone. He was there is fifteen minutes.

He removed the mouse from the apartment with ease and helped Ciara pack up her things—making little quips and remarks about her belongings as they did. They'd decided she would stay at Angelina's until the infestation was taken care of. It wasn't exactly up for discussion. When she saw the little animal, she burst into tears.

You don't have to take care of the dog while I'm here, she said, unpacking clothes onto Angelina's floor.

The cheap white blinds were pushed to the side and the heat of the summer rolled in and climbed up their bodies. It felt like a memory. Blacktop; fire-hydrant; water hose; barbecue.

Alright, he said. He would end up coming anyway.

*

Elias checked the traps at Ciara's every other day for three weeks. After he checked them, he came to Angelina's, and they walked the dog together. He'd given her his key to the place once she began staying there, and not too long after, she gave it back to him. They started taking the dog to the ballpark in the afternoons and watched the kids play baseball. It always smelled of charred meat and gasoline. Elias cited it as one of his favorite smells. A deeply nostalgic, summer smell, while also distinctly Midwestern.

The Friday of that first week, they left the dog at home and walked the entire bike trail—desperate to see where it led. After two and a half miles, it dead-ended at a lake. They took their shoes off and dipped their toes inside while sitting on a fallen tree.

I haven't seen any mice in two days now, he said, cupping water into his hands.

They're waiting for me to get comfortable again, Ciara said. It's a long con. You must know that.

You think they're that proactive? He laughed.

I do.

They lowered their bodies so they were up to their shins in the water and joked about the new dynamic they'd adopted. That he was now to her what they both were to Angelina. That this was a cycle, and when would it be his turn?

Well, what do you need? Ciara asked dipping her arms into the water.

She looked at his face; the way his skin deepened with each passing summer day and shimmered under the layer of his sweat. There was a playful silence that sat with the thin sound of the water before devolving into something much more sensual.

I don't know, he smiled, climbing out of the water. I always mix up what I want and what I need.

The second Thursday of those three weeks Jordan and Arman had an anniversary date, so she and Ciara couldn't talk on the phone. The following Thursday Ciara and Elias were watching *Sorry to Bother You.* The movie set up wasn't ideal; it was on a laptop screen ahead of them while they sat on the couch.

This was the third movie they'd watched together; right after *Johnson Family Vacation* and *Drumline.* Each time they watched a movie they'd sit there, falling into each other when something was funny—pass out on the couch and then get brunch in the morning. The first time they'd passed out on the couch, Ciara found the proximity to be uncomfortable. Too suggestive to ignore. Though, she was not opposed to the suggestion exactly, just hesitant about pursuing it. His head was on one end of the couch and Ciara's on the other. Every time this happened, Ciara woke up in the middle night, weighed the possibility of going to the bed, then stayed where she was.

The same happened that night. They fell asleep next to each other sexlessly; neither daring to move an inch once slumber had begun. Ciara wasn't sure why they continued to do this—why Elias did—but she didn't want to break the spell. She didn't want to ask. It was far too uncomfortable to have been done out of convenience but neither of them jumped at the obvious opportunity that laid dormant between them. It was possible he was indifferent toward her romantically, though she couldn't be sure. She was out of practice.

It occurred to her that he could have learned from his missteps with Angelina. Perhaps that's why she didn't act either. What she felt for certain was that they'd both previously forged connections with desperation at the forefront and that the line between nirvana and total devastation was precariously thin. It required prudence.

In the morning, Elias crept off the couch and began the coffee.

Strong, please, Ciara mumbled.

I know, he said. I know.

*

On August twentieth Ciara and Jordan talked briefly—it was Jordan's birthday. Ciara called back a few days later, but Jordan didn't pick up. When Jordan finally did call Ciara back, she was with Elias. It was a Sunday, and they were swimming in the lake. Elias had gotten a used bike for sixty dollars, and they began riding to the water a few times a week. They'd ridden there for the first time on the last day of July— drunk after Ciara brought him to a work party. They went in, fully submerged in their party clothes, and dried off as they pedaled back to the car.

Ciara swam to the dirt shore and wiped her eyes.

Do you need your goggles?

No, she said. I'm not going back underwater.

When she jumped back in they swam out as deep as they could. Deep enough that their feet couldn't touch the ground. Their heads bobbed above and Elias grabbed her legs under the water, scaring her. He had long, angular fingers that felt like flower stems on her skin. She put her arms around his neck and felt burdened with wonder.

Over Christmas, he said, gasping for air, we should go somewhere.

She played with his hair. With what money, Elias?

We could save up, he said. Go to Colorado and hike or something. We could go to Ohio for all I care. I just don't wanna stay here forever.

His eyes were shut with water; smile a mile wide; water weighing his hair down as it sponged all the moisture.

Okay. Let's go.

Ciara's ears were half in the water as Elias lowered her. She loved the cold, liquid song it made. She didn't believe a word she said. She didn't believe Elias fully did either.

Which city first? she asked. Who will watch the dog?

It got dark late at that time, and they stayed in the lake until the sun was just behind the trees to their left. They climbed out of the water and drip-dried in front of a large tree—pulling out the peaches and carrots they packed for a snack. For a moment, it seemed as if the sun would never move. Immortalize itself in statis there is their eyeline above the greenery. Then she remembered that everything wrinkles; everything bends with age and in the context of time.

Elias draped a towel over his shoulders and shook the water out of his locs. Ciara watched him solemnly. He watched her with something she could not decipher. It was an awful game they were playing.

We need to figure out what we're gonna do, Elias said suddenly.

About?

About her not coming back.

You sound so certain, Ciara laughed. She looked at the pile of their shoes, wet with residual water beneath their towels in the grass.

I am certain, he said, fingers sticky from the peach he was eating. I didn't remember this until recently, but a few weeks before she left, we'd gone to the museum for a Hopper exhibit. She was always talking about Hopper, so I got the tickets as a surprise.

He put the exposed, soft yellow middle of a peach in his mouth.

We went through the exhibit, he said, and she stood in between these two paintings for twenty minutes. Didn't say a word. After I'd left the room and come back, I pointed to one and said, She looks like you. Then she just started crying. Elias pressed his bare back against the bark of the tree behind him. She asked me if that was supposed to be a joke, and I told her I didn't know what it was supposed to be. I didn't know why I said it. She was never the same with me after that.

The air smelled fresh and alive the way the whole world does to a nine-year-old. A lightning bug circled their feet. Cicadas cried above them. Ciara could hear kids in the distance; the way a sound thins into the air the second it leaves the throat. She imagined that area and what it would look like at the end of the year—filled with snow. Frozen over.

Do you remember which painting it was? Ciara asked. Elias shook his head.

They searched "popular Ed Hopper paintings" into google and scrolled until Elias pointed.

The paintings in question were "Automat" (1927) and "Eleven A.M." (1926). "Eleven A.M." was the one he likened her to. A naked white woman sat in a mute blue chair looking out of her window with undiscernible emotion. She imagined Angelina sat like that, wherever she was in the world.

It feels strange that she's been gone for so long, and now I hardly remember the brief life I had with her, Elias told her, somehow between a choke and a laugh. When we first met, I felt such an attraction. I couldn't exactly assign the attraction at the time, but I knew it was there, in some way. I should have known it was friendship, but when we'd first spoken to each other—and I know this will sound intense—I felt like I'd be saved.

Oh God. Ciara laughed a quiet, gentle laugh. She held his bony arm soft in her hand.

Not as if I'd finally found the great love of my life—obviously, he laughed and licked his fingers clean. But there was so much I needed back then. That we both needed, and I felt like we could smell it on each other. Elias stood up and began packing away some of their things. The sun had vanished.

I knew we should've just been friends. But—you know. He averted his eyes. There's a difference between having someone to talk to and having someone to hold you. At the time—he looked to the ground—I think we both just wanted someone to hold us.

*

On Ciara's birthday in October, Elias took her to a roller-skating rink. They'd watched *Roll Bounce* recently in a fit of nostalgia, and it felt like the perfect outing. The night they watched the movie, they fell asleep in the bed. Elias wrapped his arms around her subconsciously as a motorcycle drove by.

It was 2000's night at the rink and the music made them feel like middle schoolers. They held hands as they rounded the rink; Elias skating backwards when the time allowed. Ciara snapping pictures of him. For her birthday he got her a 35mm film camera from Goodwill and a book of poems.

You're supposed to be saving your money, she said with the presents in hand. For Colorado and/or Ohio, remember?

He said, Why can't we have it all?

At the end of October, Jordan called to say the girl from the gym had gotten a new job and moved away. Her voice broke a bit when she told Ciara this. She felt they'd gotten close. She was back to square one. Jordan had talked to her mother about it—this loss—and she said it never stops happening. It never gets easier. That she'd lost many close friends in her life.

I thought about it for a while, Jordan said, and just realized—I didn't know who my mother's best friend was. Or, I guess, the thought of her having one seemed so absurd and childish. So, I just asked her who it was—if anyone at all.

What did she say?

Get this: the guy that mows her lawn. She laughed, baffled and Ciara heard the click of her lighting a candle. She was serious, too. He comes into the house and drinks coffee and eats muffins with her every time he finishes. They talk about *Law and Order* and she's helping him plan his proposal.

Is it, like, sexual? Ciara was cleaning her apartment—putting the summer clothes into boxes.

I thought so too, but no. I think they honest to God just get each other. I laughed at first, but then I felt so jealous.

Ciara took inventory of her room. Her water bottle. Elias's umbrella. A movie ticket.

What happens if he stops cutting her grass? Do you think they'd still talk?

I don't know. Jordan inhaled as if she had more to say, then she conceded: Yeah. I really don't know.

*

On November 14th, Elias and Ciara both got an envelope from Angelina that held one-hundred dollars and said that it was over. She would not be back. The lease was up and movers would be coming in ten days. They could put the dog up for adoption if they wanted. She couldn't take care of him. The last line was: I didn't envision it going on like this. I'm sorry for everything.

They analyzed the message while eating Chinese food on the floor. Ciara was in running shorts and a large T-shirt, and Elias was still in the button-up and slacks he wore to work. Ciara picked the green shirt out for him on a shopping trip a few weeks before.

They walked the dog before this, taking the long route and picking up dinner before going back to the apartment. On the walk, the two of them tried to remember who was initially in charge of Fridays. That knowledge had long since evaporated into the confines of a previous, less compelling life.

Ciara considered the envelope. The details of it; its eggshell color, the childlike bend of Angelina's writing. In the upper right corner, she examined the stamp.

She's from Charleston, right? Ciara asked. Elias told her yes. Then she held up the envelope. This is a Charleston stamp.

The implication of this hung over the room.

So, she's at home. He mulled this information over for a moment with a slow chew. And then said, as if it were obvious: Of course, she's at home.

You were right. She isn't coming back.

She thought she would though, he said. I never counted on that.

Why would she leave so dramatically just to do that?

To do what? Go home? Ciara nodded. Why does anyone go home? He said.

Ciara understood this as a question initially, then knew it intimately as an assertion. There is only one answer.

Ciara took stock of the apartment. The dog. The new kettle. Take out boxes in the trash. Elias's shoes. Her shoes. The mud stain. Chopsticks. The new candle. The barstools. Their bikes. The yellow wallpaper. The box fan. The new French press. Elias's glasses. Elias's phone. Elias's wallet.

The balcony door wasn't closed all the way from earlier when they stood on it and talked. Neither of them had ever smoked a cigarette, so they decided to smoke one together, and then never again.

Eleven minutes of my life span, she said. Gone like that.

Maybe we will go at the exact same place and time.

Ciara told him a story about when she'd gone ice-skating as a child. She'd bought skates from a garage sale in her neighborhood for just five dollars, and her mother took her to the rink the next day. The skates weren't in the best condition: rusted and blunt. So, when she naively attempted to do a jump she wouldn't have been able to land even in pristine skates, she fell back and smacked her head on the ice.

When I looked up, she said, everyone in the rink was hovering over me. Probably about forty eyes staring down. Some people's arms reached out, trying to get me up.

That would have terrified me, Elias said. He was standing next to her, cigarette wedged between his fingers, attempting to untangle a piece of hair out of one of her earrings.

Ciara watched people in the park beneath the balcony. Less people than in the summer, but many braved the oncoming cold.

I don't know, she said. It just made me feel so loved.

Now, a draft was coming into the apartment and Elias shut the door for them. Ciara watched him move around the room and thought of life as a never-ending carousel of circumstance. He gathered their used dishes, took them to the sink, and began scrubbing. The motion—the bend of the elbow and then the flexing of it—moved her.

What will we do? She asked. It was a dry croak, mechanical and foreboding.

About the dog? He asked. We'll figure it out.

She watched him at the sink, body in servile motion. His arm reaching out, then pulling in. She watched him like this for a while and never got bored. Then, she went to go be with him.

SEEING IT THROUGH

The young couple left the theater and walked to a nearby bar. Behind them, the marquee read: *Eyes Wide Shut—One Night Only.* They'd gone with some of their friends and co-workers from the library. It was an independent theater with only two show rooms, and the couple frequented it to the point of the cashiers and ushers knowing their names. On the theater's Instagram, they noted that every Friday in February they would play a different romance film in the spirit of Valentine's Day. The Friday before was a special triple feature of Richard Linklater's *Before Sunrise, Before Sunset,* and *Before Midnight.* The Friday before that, *Love & Basketball,* and the Friday before that, *In The Mood for Love.* Why they chose to end on *Eyes Wide Shut,* the man couldn't understand. He said this as he threw out the woman's empty Sprite cup. She'd hardly noticed it left her hand.

It's so funny, the woman said. Seeing them get all riled up like that. Cruise and Kidman. And they were married at the time. You think they ever argued like that?

God, no. Never. The man paused. Either never, or all the time.

The woman laughed and put a hand in his back pocket. The woman wore a long black dress with opaque black tights and an emerald peacoat. The man was in awe of her. He felt this way about her often, even if he wasn't very good at expressing it.

To me, the man continued, Tom Cruise is, like, a firecracker. I could see him exploding or being extremely Zen. He's a scientologist.

He's a scientologist, not a Buddhist.

Now the man laughed.

What do I know about scientology? It's all a big mystery. I bet they could be Zen, right? He pulled out his phone and googled: What is scientology?

What about Kidman? The woman guided him as he walked, looking down at his phone. Do you think she would be like that?

Like what? Pressed about him wanting to sleep with those girls?

Women.

Women. Wanting to sleep with those women? The woman nodded. No, I don't think so. She seems sensible to me.

Sensible, the woman laughed in a huff. Okay—what does that mean?

I mean, I think you have to be cool with a lot of things to operate in Hollywood. If her husband had a few stray thoughts about sleeping with someone else, I don't think it would bother her. Everyone does it. The man put his phone back in his pocket, having lost interest in scientology. He touched the back of the woman's neck and ran his thumb around her ear.

Oh.

The woman laughed small, then it evolved into something large, artificial, and rapturous.

What?

Nothing, she said. I just. I didn't know.

You didn't know what?

I didn't know that everyone did it. Thank you for telling me. She patted his hand kindly.

Alright, he said, aiming for playful diffusion. You're bending my words.

The man couldn't tell if they were fighting or mischievously bickering, as they often did.

You said everyone does it. I'm just repeating what you said. She reached into the man's other back pocket—the one her hand wasn't in—pulled out his lighter and a pack of cigarettes before bringing one to her mouth.

Nicole Kidman is very cool, she said, mouth tight, holding the cigarette in place.

The man dropped his hand. Stop that.

What? She teased the flame to the end as if to say, *Will I? Won't I?* before lighting it.

She is, she said again. She's very cool. So...*sensible*, she said the word as if she was making love to it. I'd gone all my life thinking that fantasizing about being with someone other than the person you love was a bit odd. But now I know everyone does it. And being okay with it isn't bizarre. In fact, it's sensible!

The woman still had her playful edge. The man had dropped his.

Okay. He said. Alright.

It was quiet as they crossed the street illegally, waiting for cars to pass. People moved around them in the dark. Couples hand in hand or walking beside each other—contactless. A girl ran home while on the phone with her best friend. A stray cat dipped into an alley.

The tail end of the woman's cigarette blazed as she inhaled. She'd never smoked before, and it felt both more and less exciting than she thought it would. The effect was more external than internal.

The couple was meeting their friends at the bar but had fallen behind when the woman went to the restroom after the movie. Their only friends in town were their co-workers, which made everything simultaneously convenient and complicated.

The couple passed a garden to their left, cold in the winter air. Blades of grass frozen into icicles.

I don't want anyone but you, the man said, quiet. There was only the sound of their footsteps.

Alright.

You know this. So, why are you doing this?

They turned a corner.

The women paused for a moment, debating her own candor.

Remember, she said, that night a couple years ago when we went out with our friends from our program to play trivia at that bar on Fifth? It was the drunkest I'd ever seen any of us. I remember David told us he felt jealous of Catholics. Ludicrous statement, by the way. But he found the concept of confession to be intoxicating. He said he just wanted to tell someone all his faults because they ate him up inside.

I think I told him to just pray, the man said, remembering this fondly. Forgetting how they got there, and where they were going.

Yes, the woman smiled. But he said that wouldn't work because he needed to *hear* the absolution. He wasn't a man of faith, though he wished he was. He got so sad at the table, we all just decided to—you know—help him. Everyone's going around saying; Oh, sometimes I have intrusive thoughts about burning my house down. I killed a frog once when I was five. I was a bully in middle school, and it still haunts me. Right? Stuff like that. I think I told everyone when I was a kid, I used to eat handfuls of baking soda.

They both laughed for a moment and the woman debated dropping it all together.

Anyways, she continued, when she regained her breath. Do you remember what you said?

The man thought for a moment. Something about a magnifying glass and ants on the sidewalk?

No, no. She said. You said: 'The first thing I do when I meet someone is assess how attractive they are to me. Sometimes I think a bit further. I can't help it. It's just what I do.'

The woman shrugged curtly, as if everything should click into place.

Okay? The man said.

Well, it didn't mean anything to me at the time. When we were friends. But then, we started dating and I'd think about it all the time. The first time I introduced you to my best friends. That bartender at the brewery we always see. The first time Emma worked with us. I'm always thinking—

I knew it. The man brought his fingers to his temples and rubbed. I knew it had something to do with Emma.

Let me finish, she said. The first time she worked with us. All that stuff I said before, too. I'm always like, he's thinking of sleeping with her.

They were close to the bar but had stopped on the street corner.

Go ahead and tell me I'm wrong, she said.

You're wrong.

She took a drag.

You told me a long time ago Nicole Kidman in *Batman Forever* was one of your sexual awakenings. She stood in front of the man, pulled her twists back and put on an airy, submissive sounding, Hollywood voice. Would you want me and only me if I looked like that? This petite white girl with shiny hair?

The man walked past her.

Christ—why would you say something like that?

The woman caught up with the man, took a drag, and the man pulled the cigarette from her fingers.

You're trying to punish me with this, he said shaking the cigarette. You've never smoked with me. Not once. Stop this.

Tell me you've never thought about sleeping with Emma. Not even intrusively.

It was one beat too long before he said, No.

The woman pulled the cigarette back to her lips and crossed the street. She took one last drag before walking through the bar door. The man followed slowly behind her.

They always took up the same back corner of the same bar after all these Friday night features. The couple usually went to see movies alone but had managed to get some of their co-workers to start going with them. Jerome, Saeed, R.J., and Emma had bought them both beers and had them waiting at the table. They took the last two seats left; the woman between the man and Jerome, and the man between the woman and Emma.

Everyone drank. The consensus was as follows: Saeed and Emma liked *Eyes Wide Shut*. R.J. and Jerome had not. The man and the woman were undecided about the matter. They talked it over while sipping on their third beers of the night. They tasted sour and tart and went to the woman's head with immediacy. She felt light, and the warmth of the man's hand on her knee made her body war with itself. She wanted to pry it off, finger by finger. She also wanted to kiss him, with her whole body, and feared if she did, she might never stop. Her love for him sometimes felt like an afflic-tion; all the operations and logical functions of her anatomy cowering to the whims of the almighty heart.

Of course, you didn't like *Eyes Wide Shut,* Emma said to Jerome. You didn't like *Before Midnight* either.

Well, they don't strike me as Valentine's Day movies, he said. They're both extremely unromantic.

Disney kids—both of you. She pointed to Jerome and R.J.

Jerome turned to R.J. with a look that said, *What's she on about?* Because Emma was always on about something.

She thinks we've been spoiled by fantasy. R.J. took a swig of his beer.

That's what romance *is*. It's seeing something through to the end—temptation—all that. The romance is in the choice. If there's no choosing what's the intrigue? Right? She pointed to the man for validation, and he played with a hangnail. Who wants to watch a movie where two people are madly in love with each other the entire time?

I'd like that movie I think, the woman said with sardonic flair; eyes squinted as if thinking hard. Everyone laughed. What? It's true.

The woman was getting theatrical now, intrepid in the face of alcohol.

That's what *Before Sunrise* and *Before Sunset* were, she said. Two people with eyes only for each other. And guess what? We all walked out of that movie on a high.

So, what—pretend the third movie doesn't exist? Emma asked.

I'm just saying it's interesting. Focused love is interesting. And it's possible.

So, you do want to pretend the third movie doesn't exist.

The woman looked at Emma; she had orangish blonde hair and a point-ed nose. The woman said: I think we're having two different conversations.

The man leaned into the woman and kissed her cheek. The woman swallowed her drink.

Personally, R.J. added, I would've stopped after the first movie.

Everyone chided him—always so naïve, so green.

It's true, he said. I mean it was interesting. Keeping the original cast, watching them age. Doing it over—what—like, eighteen years? But nothing stands alone anymore. There's always gotta be a sequel or a trilogy. It's no better than superhero movies.

You know it's better than *any* superhero movie, Saeed said. It's not the same thing. It was artistically driven, not financially.

I like when things stand alone., R.J. said. When you bottle a moment—keep it contained in its own positive ecosystem. They had it right in the first movie, all the way up to the end. Those two shouldn't have planned to meet again in six months. Said it themselves—it's doomed. Should've just held that memory as it was and carried on with their lives.

Emma rolled her eyes dramatically and then locked eyes with the man. He laughed.

How morose, she said. She was sitting in loose jeans, legs crisscrossed in her seat.

It isn't morose. Look, he said. When I was ten my twin sister started doing competitive cheer. We lived in a very strict household; limited TV and no phones until we graduated from high school. My sister practiced after school and I had to sit there, in the lobby, doing my homework until she was done because I wasn't allowed to stay home alone yet. After practice, her friends would come and talk to me. There was one girl—Aniah—who would sit and talk with me until her parents got her. She'd tell me about her school—what math they were doing, what they did in gym class. Like, her favorite music, cartoons—everything. We began sneaking notes into each other's bags and would find them randomly throughout the next day. I told all my friends from school about her, but I didn't have any evidence of her outside of the notes. Everyone was telling me she wasn't real, but I didn't mind it. It was like a world outside of my world. Then one day, when we were twelve, she just stopped showing up to the gym. My sister didn't know what happened. I think she had a bad home life. But I never saw her again.

R.J. sat back in his chair, slow, as if in a dream.

That was the first time I felt like I mattered to someone.

For a moment, it seemed he would say more, but he didn't.

Emma locked gazes with the man again. Then, they both laughed.

Emma was always looking to the man when something was funny; both the man and the woman knew it. The man pretended not to know it, and the woman knew that too.

You're not serious. Emma's face was turning red as she laughed. You don't actually think that's romantic—reminiscing on something that happened to you as a child? You think that justifies your stance?

R.J. shrugged as if to say, *Well.*

Christ, Emma chided. You're further gone than I thought.

Everyone's laughter was sonorous and thick. R.J. took it on the chin. The woman joined in, but only a little, as to not seem like the odd one out.

I'm not trying to be mean. Emma uncrossed her legs, leaned forward, then spoke slow and clear. This is all I'm saying: bottling a moment to preserve its goodness rather than seeing it through is not romantic. It is not romantic to deprive yourself of potential happiness just because you're afraid one day the happiness may fade. It is destructive and sad. Because then you're twenty-fucking-eight, she pointed to R.J., looking back on a decontextualized moment, wishing for the life of an adolescent boy with no phone.

Tell us how you really feel, Jerome said. She told him to fuck off and threw a napkin at his face.

Everyone broke into their own conversations—forgetting the topic of the movies all together. They were never going to agree. The woman talked to Jerome and R.J. and the man talked to Emma and Saeed. It had been four drinks, then. Everyone's bodies were loose; knocked unsteady by minor touches. The woman saw an expression like confusion on Jerome's face, then it transformed into a wide-eyed epiphany.

He asked Emma if anyone had ever told her she looked like Nicole Kidman before.

R.J. said he had; it was one of the first things he'd ever said to her. Saeed chimed in agreement. He hadn't noticed until then, but they were right. Maybe they needed Kubrick to steer them in the right direction.

Guys, Emma said. Really? Come on.

I see it, the woman said evenly. Don't you? She looked at the man and then pointed at Emma. I mean it's really striking.

I don't know, the man said.

Yeah, no—I see it. The nose, she said, motioning around her face. The cheekbones. The hair. The *effortless cool.*

She thinks I'm cool guys. Emma cheesed clutching her heart.

Yes, the woman said. You are. She is! The woman gestured to her; flat palm turned upwards. So carefree and laid back. You seem like nothing ever bothers you. You seem, like—I don't know, she shrugged. You seem so sensible.

The man could hear his pulse in his ears, thrumming like a snare.

Look at her, R.J. said. She's blushing.

You have to buy me dinner first, Emma joked.

I admire that about you. I should be more like that. Right? The woman looked at the man. More calm?

I just got to the point where I realized I can't control anything, Emma said casually. My partner wants to leave or cheat on me? Go ahead. I'm stuck in traffic? So be it. Waiter messed up my order? Maybe I'll like it better this way. You know. It's one of those things. Emma finished her beer and then pulled her legs back up on her chair. When I was with my ex-boy-friend, about a year in I realized I had a fat crush on his best girl friend. And I just accepted. I was like—alright. I like this girl. Everyone involved knew it. He knew it, she knew it, but what can you do about it? It was just a fact. So, we all just carried on. Then, when he and I broke up, I dated her. She laughed and ran a hand through her hair. He called me like, *I knew it, I knew it! It's always who you suspect.* And—I mean—yeah it is. But so what?

How long did you date? The man asked.

Three weeks, she said. Anyways, she was crazy.

Jerome and R.J's bodies rocked with laughter, falling into each other.

Saeed said, Bet you wished you stayed with your guy.

I did actually, she said, for a while there. But if I had, I would've just wanted to be with her. It's a double bind. Damned if you do. Damned if you don't. I'm not one for commitment anyways.

That's why you only date married people now, R.J. said.

Exactly. She raised her drink and everyone cheers-ed her.

The woman picked at her nail polish. She said, with feigned indifference: It's possible you just didn't love him if you were thinking about being with someone else while with him.

Emma looked at the woman as if she were a child. I don't think it's always that straightforward.

But it can be.

Sure, she said. It can be. But is it always?

The others had stopped listening and were talking amongst themselves. Jerome, Saeed, R.J. and the man talked about a concert they'd all went to while the woman was out of town a while ago. Emma joined in.

The woman got up to get a drink at the bar. The man stayed behind.

The man looked at Emma as she talked about the night—badgering the man about his low alcohol tolerance—and for the first time, did imagine sleeping with her. It was self-fulfilling, he decided. The woman had put it in his mind, and then he saw it. Her red hair above him like a soft, clean fabric. Her hand on his shoulder. And like that; the moment he thought about it, his interest in it dissolved. That was that. The thought of it was completely unappetizing. It was clear: nothing that was not the woman could affect him deeply anymore. He laughed quietly to himself. Maybe seeing it through in your thoughts was enough. Then a feeling in him plunged. Because now, the woman was right. He had thought about sleeping with her.

To even it out, he imagined her with Jerome. He looked more like her ex-boyfriends than the man did, and during the woman's first shift at the library, before anyone knew of her relationship, Jerome had asked her out to dinner. The man couldn't remember the details—the woman didn't get into them—but she'd rejected him kindly, and it'd never come up again.

The man hardly ever thought of this moment. The woman's devotion to him was clear.

The man imagined he was away visiting his parents and the woman invited Jerome over. He was in the man's bed. He wore the man's robe after they had taken a shower together and they both smelled of eucalyptus. Jerome had washed her hair, though the man never had. He imagined Jerome hugging her from behind—lips pressed to her shoulder.

Then the man imagined he wasn't the one imagining it, but it was the woman thinking about it all. Fantasizing about it by the man's side—vexed with want. Following this, he abruptly stopped.

The woman came back ten minutes later with a napkin in her hand and no drink. She sat next to the man, and when she did, he put his arm around her; picked up her hand—kissed the back of it. If they'd been alone, he would've stayed like that.

You disappearing on me? He said into her hand.

Sorry, she said, smile dissolving into perfectly rounded cheeks. No, I just got talking to someone.

Saeed picked up the napkin she'd placed on the table to wipe the ring around his lips, but then waved it in the air like a flag.

What's this? He said. A *numberrrr!* He sang the word like a pop song.

She's still got it, R.J. said, shaking his head.

The man looked at the woman.

Oh come on, she said. It was some kid. He was like, twenty-one and wanted to know what to do in town.

That was a line, the man said.

No, really. He was English. He's just blowing through town and needs things to do. I recommended some places to him; he bought me a drink then gave me his number, in case I thought of anything new. That was it. She put her hand on his leg.

You are dating a beautiful woman, Jerome said to the man in a taunt. I'm sure this happens all the time.

Jerome and the woman met eyes and laughed. The man looked past them, at the wall.

It does, the woman said. I usually keep it to myself. I don't want to make him uncomfortable. But it is very common. Maybe once a week.

Is that so, the man said.

The woman nodded—a smile stretched across her face. Oh yeah. I mean, everyone knows I have a boyfriend, but some people just don't care. People I know. Strangers. One time—actually, I never told you this, the woman laughed into her hand. But, on our second anniversary, when you'd gone to the restroom, the waiter told me he couldn't stop looking at me. I told him I was flattered—I didn't know what else to say. Then he was like, do you love that guy?

Saeed had beer dripping out his nose. Emma covered her mouth.

I really mean it! He was so embarrassed I could tell, but he said that he'd been thinking about speaking to me one-on-one his entire shift, and if he didn't, he'd regret it for the rest of his life. I mean, he saw it through, right? She pointed to Emma, and she nodded. Well, anyways—I said that I did love you. That you were the love of my life. And he said—the woman put on a voice—*what a lucky bastard.* After that—she pointed to the man— you came back, and I was so happy to see you.

The theatrical air of the conversation fell into something guileless. The woman's voice undulated against her will. She refused eye contact with any of them, especially the man.

I was so happy to be with you after that. It's always like that. When someone hits on me or whatever. I see you and I think—I'm so happy this, right here, is my life.

The woman was looking into her lap then.

I never want anyone other than you, she said. I can't even think about it.

When the couple left the bar, they walked home in hesitant silence. They passed a park, a church, a fountain. On their first date two and a half years before, they took a walk like this around their old university town. The man was so nervous he couldn't find it in him to reach out and touch the woman's hand. His had gone numb. It was a feeling he'd forgotten about, or that—he'd assumed—timed out by the time you left high school; a feeling rooted in juvenile beliefs about how connection should feel and how it actually does. He'd never told the woman this—or that when she finally did reach out and grab his hand, the feeling numbed his whole body. He almost tripped over his own feet. This was the truth: He hadn't thought about sleeping with anyone else in a while. He'd made up his mind about the rest of his life a long time ago.

The woman looked over to the man as they walked—saw his blank expression and wondered if she'd pushed him too far. She couldn't help it. When she went to the bar, she immediately told the guy that she had a boyfriend, as she always does. He didn't care, as they often don't. After pleasantries, the guy told her she had an aura of magnetism around her and asked if she'd like to go home with him. She shook her head slow and returned to her table. Herein lay the problem: the woman felt that she was always protecting the man from how desired she was. How, if she wasn't the dutifully devoted person she was, she could be gone.

In the house, the woman lay face up on their bed. The man made them both a cup of chamomile tea and put an extra teaspoon of honey in hers, the way she preferred. He found her legs dangling off the edge of the bed, and rubbed lotion on them, then her feet—dried crisp and cracked in the winter climate. He kissed her ankle, then her knees. The man pressed his face against the woman's shins and hugged her legs as if they were a body pillow. He felt the embrace warm on his skin. He thought, this is how it feels to love her. To be at her feet. He wanted to express this sentiment to her but doubted he could convey the intensity of the feeling. He opted for silence.

The woman felt something strange and wet on her face, then discovered she was crying. It was hushed, as if it were happening in a far-off room to someone else. She wasn't sure why it was happening.

I don't like surprises, she said. The words crumbled into the air.

I don't have anything to surprise you with.

The man stayed there, drawing with his fingers on the fleshy cushion of her calves.

You've got no clue about my feelings for you, he said.

Sometimes, the woman said, I think I want you to say terrible things to me, so we can skip to the bad part instead of it catching me off guard.

You don't know that there's a bad part.

There's always a bad part.

The man watched the woman from below and then approached her, bringing her face into his hands. She leaned her head into his palm and felt her mind go clear. He said her name and she looked up at him—the whites of her eyes lustrous in wait.

By the time the couple remembered the tea it had gone cold. The woman went to take a shower and the man read a book from the library in bed. In the shower, the woman discovered she forgot her towel. The man noticed before she did and set it on the bathroom sink without a word. When the woman came out to the towel waiting for her, she thought she'd imagined the forgetting all together. The man didn't even remember getting up from the bed.

CODA

Forgive me for breaking the silence. I know we don't operate like this, but the fifteenth is approaching, and I don't want to waste your time.

I'll just say it: I moved back a month ago. It was Elijah's idea. I was vehemently against it—I want to make that clear. It was a sensitive subject as his sister is here, and she is sick, and my only real rebuttal was that you are here, too. Though, in the end I hid behind my disdain for returning to our hometown in our thirties. As you can see, I lost.

I write all that to say, I saw Genevieve at the grocery store the other day. It was the first time I had seen her in about ten years. I never told you this, but I have you both muted on social media. (I know it sounds harsh but trust me, it's more for my own sanity than it reflects my feelings towards either of you.) So, I hadn't known she'd cut her hair, and I hadn't known she was pregnant again. Two years ago, on our day, I remember you said you may try again, immediately followed by a sigh and your pointer finger flirting with the circumference of my resting hand. The truth comes out now: I loved that you didn't want it. It was helium to my bloodstream—I could've floated away.

When confronted with the sight of her round stomach, I first felt a prickling betrayal, followed by a rush of shame. It came to me then that we may be sick people.

The boys were there with her—Josiah's hand on her pant leg as a distraction while Coleman snuck a cereal box into the buggy right as they were checking out. I have to ask—did you teach him that? It only worked when we did it to your mother because she couldn't care enough to engage with the hassle of putting it back. Genevieve just said, Again? And set it on top of the gum display at checkout. I did laugh to myself thinking of how defeated we would've been if your mother had been so callous when we were that age. Maybe we'd be more disciplined now if we didn't always get our way.

I had a dream the night after I saw your family, though it felt more like déjà vu. It was a reimagining of your eighteenth birthday. All the same, but the sky was canopied in unnatural purple light. The house was yours but looked more like where we went to kindergarten. Those small chairs, the window that only the gym teacher could open. The display with the colored cards to say who was good and bad.

In the dream, I hadn't brought Nita with me because she didn't work a shift with me that day. And because I never brought Nita, she never called Genevieve to pick her up. Which means Genevieve never came into the house, you never spilled your drink on her, and you never cleaned it off her alone in the downstairs bathroom. All the other major events remained. Your brother still broke the good chair with Chanelle on his lap. Anya and Caleb still made the dip that gave everyone food poising. We still ran through the entirety of *Lover's Rock* as people began to file out, but instead of being in the bathroom when "All About Our Love" played, you were by my side. We were the only two left. We sang to each other while placing ceramic plates in the trash—while throwing glass cups at the wall—watching the shards fall down for our entertainment, catching the light like sharp prismatic rain. When the song ended your hand found my lower back and you didn't move it. The sun was just outside the window, knocking on the glass, waiting to swallow us whole. You had a look I'd never seen you wear in all my life. It was scared, but somehow sanguine. Skin melted off your face in a slow, waxy drip. Then, you turned to me and said with a tremor, What are we doing?

When I woke, Elijah said I was shaking. I told him it was a reoccurring nightmare from my childhood.

I do not dream of you often. I hadn't in a long time; I don't think my body could handle it. When I did it was only in flashes—never so vivid. Never reaching into my chest with such determination, ringing my bones like a bell. I feel I've awoken from a deep sleep.

There was something about seeing your kids kick around that grocery store. Coleman's eyes were as big as you said they were—just as brown and glossy as yours. Hungry for mischief. Already attuned to what is owed to him; what he can bend to his will. Seeing you once a year has always allowed me this distance. I often forgot how real and delicate your life was. When I left the store, I dry heaved into the open air of my Camry.

I'm writing to let you know we've reached the end of the line. I don't feel it's up for discussion. I find our friendship has become indecent. And while it has never been physical, I'm sure you can agree with me that this is not entirely innocent. There has always been deception in the ambiguity of our relationship. I think we need to be honest with each other.

Do you remember that first year out of college when we saw each other at Anya and Caleb's wedding? You and Genevieve were on a break, still unmarried. Elijah and I hadn't reconnected yet. That was the longest we'd gone without seeing each other since ninth grade when you moved to Ohio for a year, then moved back. I didn't know if you would come to the wedding because you'd stopped speaking to me. When I'd call your place Genevieve would say you were out, but on the days you picked up you sounded miles away. A voice in a vacuum—asking questions as though to fulfill a duty. Nothing about you felt corporeal.

When you walked through the church doors at the wedding—and this is absolutely true—I watched my life flash out before me in a sepia glow. There had never been a longing that took the reins of my life with such bite. I don't know how else to put it. I would've lit myself on fire for you.

You have to understand that in those days I was always trying to understand the unsaid. I decoded your every word, every move, in case you were like me—mute when faced with the opportunity for confession. The hug you gave me after our eyes met felt prophetic. As though it was a long time coming and your weary clock had run out of steam. You said my name in my ear with the determination of a child's first word. I was so certain of you. There had always been an idea about us, and it lingered with weight every time we were together. *Is this the time? Will we be honest now?*

It's been near eight years since that night in your hotel room when you proposed we see each other once a year if nothing else—make the arrangements for the next time a year in advance. I see now that the "nothing else" was no more than false assurance. Life was about to begin.

When you said it, your head was in my lap and your top lip was shiny with champagne. You did not mention the silence, so I let it be. There were other things to attend to. Your mother was moving away. You missed your innocence. You missed the shed—we'd made ours by the lake as children, with blankets and Gameboys and board games that had become water soaked and flimsy. You missed independence. You missed selfishness. You missed New Years with my family in our old neighborhood. When you asked how my sister was—asked if she had a better taste in women now—I told you to come around and find out. That's when you got quiet.

I thought you'd fallen asleep—your breathing was so still—but then you said: If Genevieve never comes back, I think I'll be alright. I prayed for her disappearance and wished myself a witch. Then you uttered the most naïve sentence I'd ever hear: Have you ever considered the possibility of us?

Your hair was my favorite then—kinky on the top, tapered on the sides. No ear piercings yet, skin inkless. I told you I had considered us; that everyone had. You must have known that. The way people were so cautious around you and me when they liked one of us. People in school treated us as an inevitability.

You told me Genevie had always considered us, too and confessed that was partially why we'd gone so long without seeing each other. I'll never compromise on you again, you said.

Genevieve did come back, of course. I understand that some compromises must be made—it is the nature of love—but it took me a long time to forgive that I wasn't invited to your wedding. I have held onto this animosity for so many years and I finally feel removed enough from the pain to be honest about it. Hindsight has allowed me to accept that my feelings towards the matter were based on principle. If I had been invited—though I would have gone—I would not have wanted to be there. I may have walked out. I may have objected. (I played through that scenario many times, but even in my daydreams I couldn't see it going my way.)

I want you to know I get why you implemented the rule of the year long silence—I know Genevieve has no tolerance for our friendship. The thing is, I think it only made things more intense. The meetings became a sort of beacon for me. Before Elijah, nothing in my life could compare to what I felt on those days. I lived in a yearlong hibernation—only in your presence able to breathe.

The third meeting after your wedding—the year we met in New York—that's when I knew this was jeopardous. You didn't mention Gen or the baby once—do you realize that? For the first hour I tried to determine whether this move was calculated or genuine, then I gave it up. It didn't matter. I reveled in their absence. My love for you had always had a narcissistic heart.

The whole night was a nostalgia fest—that's what our entire love has been. Pictures from our families on vacation together. A photo you drew of me in the shed during a thunderstorm that is always in your wallet. You pressed your hand to mine, collapsed the space between our fingertips and asked me if I'd ever grow. Must you always take care of me? You said this friendship keeps you alive with a warm hand to my cheek, a stroking thumb, and I knew we were both kidding ourselves. I knew we were putting our whole lives at the mercy of our present desires. And still, I slept next to you in that bed. It doesn't matter that we didn't touch. That we were stiff and separated by the open space of the king mattress. I knew I would keep choosing this life if never presented with a way out.

In the morning as I packed my things, you grabbed my wrist. Please don't go, you said. I don't want to return to life just yet.

I have always been so desperate for you; so shamelessly desperate for you, that in that moment I felt what you must always feel. The live heart of another, pulsating in my hand.

When we played house, you would get upset when I stuffed pillows in my stomach and said I was with child. (Back when we thought pregnancy was a result of the magic kiss at the altar). You always insisted you didn't want kids, even the year before you had one. Then, that was your life. And still, you wanted to remain with me, untouched, in a hotel that was not home to either of us.

I ruminated on this concept for a long time. The thought that you loved me more than your own offspring. That, perhaps, I knew your true desires more than your own wife. I felt it romantic and profound. I'd roll it around in my head like clay—molding visions of a life I'd never know. Only now does the thought strike me as sad.

I think life will be easier for us both if we accept that a conventional friendship is not possible.

When you asked me a year ago if I really loved Elijah, if this life is what I want, I was being honest when I said yes. I know we used to make fun of him in high school. He was so demure—so reserved. I had no idea he had also moved to Denver. When he messaged me asking about the book I'd just posted, and then asking for dinner, my natural inclination was to say no.

How wrong we both were. How wrong I've always been.

All those lofty desires that had gathered dust in my mind—he fulfills them. The other morning, I was bedridden from period pains and he brought breakfast to me on an oak platter. On my birthday, the living room was a shrine of balloons and roses. He talks me down from every ledge. He brings grace to every disagreement—a calm to all chaos.

A few nights ago, we realized we both kept journals in college and decided to read through them together. What trust. I mean really, how deeply vulnerable. Towards the middle of the night, he read an entry where he mentioned an ex-girlfriend of his. I don't remember it verbatim, but she had an M name and it said something like: We haven't been together in five years and still she is the first thing I think about in the morning and the last thing I think about at night. I think I'll always default back to her.

We laughed and I joked about how he can leave me if he wants. We aren't married after all. He said, I felt more for you in the first week than I felt for her in all those years.

It was a lifetime ago. It was resolved. Yet, in the shower the next morning, my heart was uprooted. Isn't it harrowing how one's love can move from room to room; with each move, the purehearted belief that *this* is the last one? He had felt that certainty before. And to stay in that one room for five long years, even while distanced from the lover—it terrified me. I sat down, let the water whip me, and I wept—only getting up when I smelled the breakfast he was cooking in the kitchen. It was clearer to me then than it ever was; he has every fragment of my love.

I've found that the promise of you was always more enticing than the reality. Limbo provided such security. It was a good ruse on our part, meeting all these years in secret under the pretense of being best friends. Getting on an airplane to maintain a 'platonic' connection your wife so ardently detested it had broken up your relationship once before. Nothing good has ever required from me this level of discretion.

I had grand visions of you all my life—now hazy and foreign, played out in cinemascope. I saw us walking down the street. I saw us hiking a tall mountain. I saw us as sea creatures lounging in a big shell. I saw my fingers in your mouth and you were sucking like a baby. I saw a baby in your arms with brown prodding eyes. A candle in your hand. My back hot and wax soaked. Your teeth in my jaw, hungry. I saw dinner on the back patio. Our mothers sat by the Christmas tree. A full kitchen sink. A portrait. A foyer wall.

When we met last year, I spent the entire day wishing I was home. It's all gray now.

Why didn't we just do it? What actually stopped us?

Maybe the intrigue was in the restraint—the fact that it would never be realized. I do believe there is an inherent romance within two people that have known each other all their lives, subtext lingering between them. I also believe that if we'd seen it through, we may have found that neither of us is what the other needs. This allegiance we have to each other—I think it will destroy the joy in our lives.

In the hotel room—the night of Anya and Caleb's wedding—you said in your best Jack Twist impression, I can't quit you. I laughed and told you I would never try.

I don't know everything. You imagine the life ahead of you—try to be one person and come out the other side weathered. Things get muddled in the fray and time is at a full sprint. Door closed after door closed and there we were, tight fisted, trying to jam one open. I like to be welcomed into a room. Can't you see it now? There's nothing left for us here. The party is over. Everyone's gone and we're the only ones that remain. We're toying with the fever of the sun. Save your life before it's swallowed up. I'm going to save mine.

TO BE KNOWN

When I walked into the living room, the first thing I heard was Maida saying that she was not beautiful anymore— that she never wanted to be again. She said it while taking a drag—blowing the white smoke into the face of the guy next to her. She said, beauty is palatability through the male gaze and she didn't care for males gazing at her. The guy smiled and sipped his wine. The rest of the guests laughed. When someone asked what she was if not beautiful she said, everything else. Tantalizing. Wouldn't you prefer to be that, she asked. Tantalizing? It's like a lightning strike to your chest.

The room was warm. Eucalyptus oil diffused quietly; the intrusion of nicotine scratched at my nose. Maida and the guy resided on the couch, splayed drunkenly on opposing ends; wine in one hand, cigarette in the other, dying out. She had her thrift store pearls around her neck, a stained blue button up, and black dress pants. Barefoot. The others were on the floor or in chairs—fighting to be the dominant voice of pretension in the room as Angel Olsen's "Spring" crooned in the undertow.

That's because you see beauty as precision or warmth, when in reality beauty is alarming. Right? I read that somewhere, I think.

This friend—Irene—was sitting in her boyfriend's lap in a maroon armchair by the window—her heeled feet hanging over the edge. The people seated at her feet hummed in agreement. Her boyfriend said they'd read it in *The Secret History*.

Right, Irene said. As long as someone looks at you and feels disarmed, you are always going to be beautiful. Doesn't matter what you call it.

Maida was displeased with this. Her eyes found me in the doorway of the bedroom.

Salem, she said. Do you think you're beautiful?

The guests turned towards me.

Do I think I am, or do I think people think I am?

Maida shrugged.

I don't know, I said. I don't know how people see me.

Maida turned to the man next to her, who was already looking at me. The red wine splashed over her glass's edge, onto the white fabric of the couch. Though, no one seemed to care.

What do you think, Theo? Are you disarmed by her?

Theo continued to look at me cautiously, considering me in quick blinks of his lashes. He gave a very subtle part of the lips—an answer brewing—then, turned his nose down into the echo chamber of his wineglass and said in a single, honest, airy breath: Yeah—yes.

Of course, he would say that, Maida said to the room. He thinks with his eyes.

Everyone erupted into a thin drunken laughter. Including him—including me.

I found the wine sitting on the middle shelf of a bookcase by the window—on top of *Bluets* and *Giovanni's Room.* I poured it into my glass and pulled a chair to the only open space, next to Theo.

Everyone was huddled over one of the guest's phone as she swiped through a dating app; what I assumed prompted the discussion of beauty, because—objectively—not many people on the app had it. She launched into a story about a bad first date where the guy cried about his ex-girlfriend next to her on a park bench. This drew a deep guttural laugh from Maida. When the calm returned, she introduced me as her friend from home.

She just flew in a few hours ago, she continued. She's going to be moving in with me.

Where were you before? Irene asked.

Michigan. In my childhood bedroom. New York before that.

Don't ask her about New York, Maida said, in a barely discernable slur. She won't want to get into it—won't even talk to me about it.

I had not seen Maida since our college graduation four years prior. A month before this night she and I had run into each other in a grocery store by our old high school. We trembled meat-side in the freezer aisle. It was Christmas eve. When she'd seen me, she asked how long I'd be in town. I said, for the foreseeable future. She said, you're not going back up to New York? I told her things didn't work out.

When I asked her what she was doing she said everything. I didn't know what that meant but I told her I was jealous. That I was doing nothing—in it's truest and most barren form. She asked me if I was at least happy, and I told her I'd never been more depressed.

When Maida asked me to come live with her in LA, I laughed. Then she said, No, I'm serious.

We hadn't been close in a very long time; though when we were, it was an intoxicatingly co-dependent friendship that made us find any-one outside ourselves useless. Tumultuous at its best. Always sponta-neous. When I confessed I didn't have any money for that she told me that's the whole reason why she's inviting me. If she asked, she could get Theo to help me.

Wine stained Maida's shirt in a Rorschach blotch—bleeding through and onto her tan skin. She announced that the only good thing that had ever come from her being beautiful was meeting Theo. I looked at him when she said this and watched him push his black hair back.

He turned to me.

She loves to embarrass those closest to her. Does she not?

I nodded.

He had brown skin and a mole under his left eye. When I didn't respond he turned back to the conversation.

She dived into the story of their meeting. Maida had only met Theo, she explained, because she was still beautiful back then.

I still wore dresses and brushed my hair, she laughed.

She had been in Venice Beach visiting Irene. The two of them went to a bar and Maida got stuck with the tab when Irene disappeared with someone. It was higher than she thought it would be. The guy next to her offered to pay it and she declined. He said, really, it's no problem. I can see this is troubling you. She told him she had a boyfriend, and at the time she did. She made a faux barfing noise at that detail—being with a man. Then he said, Is your boyfriend going to pay it? And soon after, I don't want anything from you. Really. So, she let him. She let him walk her home as well and they talked like they'd grown up together. When he asked if he could come in, she said no. Hard to get, he laughed. This isn't a game, she told him. You'll never have me.

The next morning, he sent her $100 over the phone and asked if she wanted to get brunch. She did.

An embarrassed smile fell calm on his lips. The others teased him.

Ah—I like beautiful women, anyways. It never would've worked, he joked, a little at his own expense.

Everyone bantered amongst themselves. Maida added that in the end she won.

He still pays for everything, she said. This apartment. This wine. These clothes. It's all him—and now he's my dearest friend. Imagine that.

A guy that had been mostly quiet throughout the night said earnestly, I always wondered why you do it. Maida's head was thrown back over the couch, speaking into the ceiling.

Fuck if I know, she said. I think he's punishing himself.

Theo's neck craned back to me, as if we've always confided in each other.

We should put her to bed, shouldn't we?

It was inside a laugh. Our eyes lingered a moment before I agreed. I wondered how long I could push the silence, and what he might do to fill it. But I said, Yes. Then, he delicately took the empty glass from my hand, placed the stem between his fingers, and carried both of ours to the kitchen sink.

*

Once the house was empty, Theo and I laid Maida in the white sheets of her bed. She mumbled something about an oil diffuser. He clicked on the one by her bedside. Once her breath was steady and low in a snore, we crept back into the living room.

I watched him gather a black jacket from the closet—stretching an arm through the narrow sleeve. With his back turned for a moment, I got to study him. He looked younger than I'd expected him to be, his skin polished.

My eyes found him finding me.

It's unfortunate that nap took you out for most of the night. The journey did you in, huh?

I'm frankly just a sleepy person.

Right, he smirked. Well, I'm going. Maida has everything—my cards, cash. If you need anything at all you'll call me, yes?

I nodded.

Good. Okay.

He looked at me, stationary in the room. When I said nothing, he said Okay playfully to himself one last time and made his way out of the apartment.

Maida was gone when I woke up the next day. The sky light over the bed burned me awake until I climbed out and drew myself a bath. The apartment wasn't grand by any means—livable for the two of us. The day washed away as I read in the bath, then on the balcony, then on the couch, shuffling Maida's Lazy Day playlist the whole day.

*

You didn't leave once?

We were eating dinner. She shoveled the penne I made into her mouth. I shook my head. I can't bear to stay in one place.

What do you do all day? I asked.

She said she often volunteered on a farm—took painting classes. Would read in parks or sit on the beach. Whatever, really.

A baby goat was born on the farm today, she said. It was so striking but I couldn't watch. I hid behind the barn until it was over.

After she went to a lookout peak and read half of some book in one sitting. She said looking out over the land, thinking about the goat, thinking about the book; she was so happy she cried. She said, I felt a bit like you.

Like me?

You're very emotional. Her silver hair was haphazardly done up in bobby pins. And yet, she said, you're so stubborn. Theo is the same way. It's because you're Tauruses. You both drive me crazy.

We went to bed at two that morning and talked in the darkness about the lost four years. She lived in Michigan while I was in New York. Maida wanted to save enough money to move to Chicago and teach. Then, she realized she didn't want to teach at all.

If I hadn't come to visit Irene in Venice that summer I don't know where I would be, she said.

I asked her about Theo. She said in some ways he is one of the closest friends she's ever had, though never anything more. She explained how things worked—the money he would transfer to her, now us, at the start of every month. She held onto his credit card for emergencies, though, there never were any. If there was anything big, all we had to do was ask and he would take care of it.

I don't abuse it, she said. I just want enough to live life. That's all.

She told me she doesn't know why he does it, but she's grateful he does.

Closer friend than me? I asked, delayed, because I had to.

Close, but no. No one could be more anything than you.

We fell asleep just before sunrise.

I went with her the next day. We met up with her friend River and helped them paint their bedroom green while listening to NxWorries. Mostly, I watched them sidestep around each other, teasing paint on the other's skin. When we started to leave Maida asked if they were going to be at Theo's for dinner that night.

Of course, they said. I love how nonchalantly he lets us commandeer his house.

It was only a few of us—Irene, her boyfriend, Maida, River, Theo, and me. He had a round wooden table in his sunroom. The wine was passed around as River brought up the latest scandalous thing Kanye West said.

We hate him, they said, But if he shuts up, what would we do?

Maida said, Be at peace for once.

I took a crab cake in my mouth and let it soak into my tongue. It was Kanye until it was Taylor Swift. Until it was Morrisey, until it was the President. Somewhere between Taylor and the President, Theo had walked away and not returned. The volume raised. Irene and Maida attempted to outdo each other in wits as River gazed at them, charmed.

I'm sorry if it's a lot, Irene's boyfriend whispered to me. We just really love to argue.

I said I didn't mind at all, I just needed some water, then got up and walked in the house.

When I walked in Theo was wiping down the countertops and listening to music off the television. He looked up.

Need a breather?

You all drink so much. I don't think I've ever met anyone that drinks the way you all do.

He instinctively ran a cup under the faucet then handed it to me.

It's a bad habit. I've been trying to get everyone to ease up, but.

He continued cleaning. I stood by the countertop watching him.

How do you find life here? He asked.

I took a sip. In the one day? Nice.

Yeah?

Yeah. I used to think I enjoyed order in some way. If I had been unemployed for a period, I would get excited at the prospect of going into work. Now I realize that I don't want to do anything at all. If all I ever did was sleep, eat, and laugh with friends every day I could die contently at fifty. Maybe even younger.

That's a funny thing to say. His tone was always warm, flirting with intrigue. Teeth creeping between his lips.

Do you enjoy work?

I hardly do anything, really. I mean that. I'm not being humble.

You're pretty young, I said despite myself, for such money.

This got him to look at me. A slight grin. Nothing seemed to faze him, only amuse him.

Am I?

Or maybe I don't know what age you are when you can afford things beyond yourself. Maybe it doesn't really exist. Not for everyone, at least.

Well, it's nepotism money. That helps. He had an embarrassed grin.

I see, I see, I chided. He smiled—looked into the sink. I thought white people made up our nepo baby market. How'd you get in there?

It helps if you were adopted into a white family as well.

There was an empty water glass in my hand. He grabbed it, refilled it, and then sat on the couch in front of the TV. He said, Come here.

When I sat down, he told me he grew up in Arkansas. That he was adopted from Guatemala as a baby and his family moved to LA when he was five. His family owns a television production company. The job was handed to him five years earlier when he was twenty-five.

But it's not like I'm building houses or teaching, or anything, he said. As far as work goes it's just kind of... He didn't seem to find the word he was looking for and just sipped his wine.

I'm twenty-five and I'm doing nothing.

I thought we just established that doing nothing is ideal.

He offered his wine glass to me and I took a sip.

We sat on the couch talking for the next hour. When a song I knew would come on I would tease him about its quality, even if I did like it. He was easily embarrassed, and I liked knowing I could embarrass him, or that he allowed me the luxury of thinking I could. He said I'm very particular, and I told him Maida would say it's because I'm a Taurus. He said, I am too, what does that say about me? I scratched my head as if to say, Well... Which, made him snort involuntarily. In the midst of his hilarity, his palm grazed my thigh without committing, then returned to it's home at the stem of his wine glass.

Shortly after, Father John Misty's album *God's Favorite Customer* began to play. I let out a humored groan.

You enjoy doing this to me, he said, turning it up.

It's not that I don't like it. I just find the album a bit desperate is all.

Hm. You're right. He closed his eyes and rested his head on the couch. That might be why I like it, he said. I'm quite a desperate person.

When I didn't say anything, he opened one eye and looked at me.

Sorry, he said. I'm a bit drunk as well.

That's okay.

Had you pegged me as one?

Not at all. Although now I'm curious to know if you are punishing yourself as Maida says.

At this moment everyone came in from outside. River was carrying Maida on their back and the others brought in the glasses and plates. Maida called for me to grab my things, that we were leaving.

You should come back tomorrow if you want, he said softly, to me only. I'll leave a key under the mat.

Okay—sure.

I thanked him for dinner and walked out with the others.

Maida returned to her farm the next day. I got a takeout brunch and read in the lush of the Descanso Gardens before getting bored and calling a car over to Theo's house. The key was under the mat as he said. He was still at work when I arrived and I spent my time going through his things, thumbing through the vinyl in his office. An eclectic mix of New Wave bands and musical soundtracks. There was a dark wooden desk in the middle of the room with gold handles on the drawers. Open on top of it was some book on solitude, and in the margins of a paragraph he wrote:

There's comfort in the fact that your thoughts only exist within you—only you have access to you in this way. And at the same time, it's a reminder that you can't ever truly be known? because every corner of you can't be scrubbed.

After reading his comment a few times, I went in the living room and watched *Death Note* on his couch until I fell asleep.

Around six o'clock I jerked awake to the sound of the front door closing and his dress shoes hard against the wooden floor.

He scanned me. You're here.

Was I too early?

No, no. It's nice to come home to someone. He began to undo his tie and walked into the kitchen.

Are you okay with pajeon?

I nodded. How was your day?

I sat on the kitchen island as he whisked flour and eggs together. He told me about a meeting he was in and talked about statistics in a way I didn't care to understand. He said he had the leftovers from dinner for lunch and they tasted better that way—after time. As Theo talked, he took a shrimp on a fork and brought it to my mouth.

How is it? He asked.

I composed myself before saying, Yeah. It's good.

He went back to talking and I listened intently. All his words were expensive and deserved their real estate. My hand reached over into the pan and picked a shell out of the mix before it was too late.

See, he said. I knew I needed you here.

Theo asked me what I was like growing up. I told him I grew up in the suburbs and went to private school my whole life.

My condolences, he laughed, because he had too. Was it miserable for you as well? He asked.

I said yes. To be "of color" in an all-white setting was a daily war, especially in your formative years when your brains busy developing schemas about life and standards and beauty. About the good and the bad and who is worthy of what. We bonded over the fact that our hells had the same fire. That that time in our adolescence probably changed us much more than we were able to pinpoint; chipping at us in subconscious, Freudian ways.

Theo wondered if I got asked to school dances a lot, and I laughed very hard before saying, No. Not once.

That surprises me. You're so likeable.

Thanks, I said. But you know how it is for black girls in places like that.

He nodded. I hope it never got to you. I smiled and turned off the eye for him, knowing it had, and in some ways, it still did.

Around ten the wine began to fog our eyes. We had said we wouldn't drink, but the hand reaching for the glass is muscle memory. We sat in his garden as he played Blood Orange's "Chosen" out of the muffled speaker of his phone. My throat ached from talking—my cheeks were strained from my seemingly permanent elation. During dinner he told me that I smiled a lot. I said, only sometimes.

Can I ask you something?

Sure. He pushed his finger around the edge of the wine glass and it sang.

Why did you ask me to come over?

He hummed. I don't know, he said. I just liked talking to you.

I thought maybe you were ready to confess.

Confess?

Your desperation.

Ah—yes. That. You want to know if I'm punishing myself, he laughed.

Are you?

What do you think? He appeared entertained, as always.

I pursed my lips to stifle a smile and looked to the ground.

I think you want to tell me.

We were sitting in two chairs facing each other. His hands tugged at the silver necklace around his neck. His skin was soft in the light coming in from the house—clean under the moon. I felt the drink falling through the cracks in my bones like rain into the gutter.

All remaining bits of façade rolled away, slowly, as eyebrows became unclenched.

I find I'm not very good at balance.

He let it hang. When I didn't fill the silence, he continued.

And I enjoy being needed, he said. Maybe more than I love, when I have loved.

I see.

Whenever my desire for being needed co-exists with love in a romantic relationship, it always falls apart. My ego always gets in the way.

So, you allow yourself to be exploited. To fulfill your neediness but to punish yourself without the connection.

I'd say Maida and I exploit each other. That's probably why it works. She's also my closest friend, though. Theo sighed and smiled as he rubbed an eye. He said, I guess it's very complicated.

There was a long silence.

I read the comment you wrote. In that book on your desk.

He played with the dials of his watch. And?

Is that what you want? I asked. To be known. Have all your corners scrubbed.

Doesn't everyone?

I tilted my head and raised my eyebrows in defeat.

I feel like I live in a loop, though, he said. I make the same mistakes every time. So, I don't—yeah. I don't know. It feels reckless to try to be known when I know how selfish I can be.

I wanted to say, you're trying to be known right now, that's why you're talking to me. And I want to know you, that's why I'm here. But I didn't say anything. I closed my eyes and listened to the music.

When I opened them after the song ended, he was already looking at me, carefully. Softly, but intensely, like I was a dying puppy.

What?

Will you tell me about New York?

The night was blue-black. An ambulance drove by and reminded me I was alive. I would have evaded him, but his own fleshy wound was wide open and breathing between the two of us.

I sat up straighter.

I was with a guy for awhile. I followed him to New York and we lived together for a bit. We butted heads, then I left.

How long did you date?

I hesitated, then said, He was never my boyfriend.

Right. He said it like he didn't want to.

I wanted him to be. But he was never going to. We had a big blow-up about it right after we had sex for the last time. I had told I loved him. It just slipped out and he asked me why I would say that.

Theo scooted a little closer and his knee touched mine.

I said, I don't know why I said that. He said, You're in love with me? And I was like, well, yes. We've been together a long time. We live together. You asked me to live with you. Do you not love me? And he started making cereal in the middle of the whole thing, saying, I don't know, I don't know. Fuck, Salem, why would you say that?

My face grew hot and sticky. Another ambulance came.

And then, I gathered as many things in my bags as I could and drove home. I left all my art on the walls. Some of my shoes. My toothbrush.

I didn't know I was crying. All the wine was wringing out of my body and my skin was melting off its bones. Then, everything was black because, I guess, my eyes were closed. It was just black, then black and warm as his arms wrapped around me. He pulled me into him. I cried into his neck as he rubbed my back fast and hard. He asked if Maida knew, and I said that nobody knows. It's very embarrassing.

As I cried, my nose was on his neck. I'd had the intrusive thought to bite it, softly, because I like the warmth of proximity. Meaningful proximity. I understood how quickly he and Maida got close then. His voice was low and gentle. I wanted to lay down inside its tides like a sensory deprivation tank.

I cried so long and hard that my body went limp. Like a baby after a tantrum—burnt out from their own erratic emotion. It all swam out of me.

I did not bite him.

He carried me into his room, put me under the covers, and turned out the light—thumbed some tears off my cheek and went to sleep on the couch.

When I woke up there was the smell of food: potatoes and onions— burning. It was almost satisfying. When I walked into the kitchen Theo was there, hovering over the stove in a white T-shirt and black running shorts. He looked at me with an apprehensive glow in his eyes.

I began to open my mouth. I must have looked quite sullen—eyes still puffy and blown. He just softly shook his head, motioned for me to pick up a plate of food, and then we walked into the garden.

When we ate, if it got too quiet, he would rub my back gently. I was quiet mostly.

I'm sorry, I said.

He shook his head. Salem.

I know but. That was a lot.

We both had things to say. He rubbed my back then squeezed my shoulder. And then, as if a confession: You're very easy to talk to.

We laughed a bit. He told me I looked very glowy, and I said it's because

I wiped my tears all over my face. Is that so? You should patent it, he said. After digging into him again for that Father John Misty album, he said I could stay if I wanted, but he had to go to work.

No that's okay, I told him. I should go home anyways.

When he drove up to Maida's and my apartment, I tried to hand his house key back to him.

Keep it. Just show up—whenever.

He leaned over through the space in front of me in the passenger seat and opened my door from the inside.

When I walked inside Maida was doing yoga in the living room.

Where the fuck were you, she said playfully. And then after looking at me a bit closer, Have you been crying?

The days began to fold into each other. Farm. Painting. Dinner. I took up running again—the air electric. Thursday nights were drunken. Fridays were hazy. There was always brunch on Sundays, usually at Irene's. She and her boyfriend flipped pancakes while Theo walked me through the French press process. River and Maida would make runs for what was missing. When the debates would pick up, Theo and I would go for a walk or shoot humorous glances across the table.

I used my key incessantly and Theo began to expect me. Some days I would cook in his kitchen until he came home so he could smell my presence from the garage. I thought I could condition him to crave me when hungry—convince him my company was as vital as food, shelter, and water. Other days I would fall asleep in his garden and wake up to his shadow overcast, eager. He never touched me. Instead, we would laugh at the television, or he would read books aloud to me. There was a week when he read Keats's *So Bright and Delicate* to me in the afternoons. When I didn't think he did it with enough conviction, I would take over and he would let me. He would let me do whatever I wanted—he handed that power over blithely.

Other days I spent with Maida, when she wasn't out of the house.

We would hike and shop. We'd taken up skateboarding—dumped it a month later. The days she spent with Theo became days for the three of us. The days I spent with him were just he and I. There was a tension in her goodbyes as I left for his home all on my own, but it was a tension we intended to ignore as much as possible. Some days she and I would attempt to paint each other—posting the botched artwork on our socials after. Or days she would talk about missing her cousins in Turkey she had not seen for years. Some days we would treat ourselves, past the means of "just enough to live" and eat a dinner that's cost went into high triple digits. We ate those dinners slowly and held the food on our tongues for longer than needed. On these days we would wonder how long we could keep this lifestyle up—living life without the imposition of work, the stress of money. One night I asked Maida if we lived in a bubble, if what we were doing wasn't real life.

With sushi in her mouth she said, This might be the realest life anyone's ever had.

We weren't always together. Occasionally, I could hear her on the phone with Theo in the kitchen while I was in the room. These days I had to confront the fact that they were also friends, even if in a different way. That they had a relationship outside of me. Despite my desire to have his attention all to myself, it was a complexity I had to be okay with.

There were other instances when Maida would disappear for days at a time, returning either entirely despondent or in complete nirvana. On the good days she would say things like, There's so much I want to tell you, Salem. And I will, I will. She would check out of conversations with a dumb grin on her face and kiss my hand before leaving the house. On the bad days she would take hour long showers with scolding hot water. When I would ask if she was okay she would say, lowly, There's something wrong with me, I think.

On the days I didn't see Theo he would send me funny Pitchfork reviews or links to earrings and books he thought I'd like. His favorite review was of Miles Kane's *Coup de Grace*. Pitchfork gave it a 3.6 and lays into his exploitation of Alex Turner in the opening lines. He sent me a voice memo of him laughing so hard he teared up. At the end of it, he said in an airy voice, I didn't even listen to the album. I just hate Miles Kane.

If I was away more than five days in a row, he would text me something like: Have you lost my key? Where have you been?

Some days I would stay away long just so he'd beg for me.

On one of the bad days in March he came over for dinner with just me and Maida. I made us slow-cooked steak fajitas and we ate on the balcony. He was wearing a red silk button-down shirt and I'd worn something similar.

You're spending too much time with me. I fear we're becoming too much alike.

As if you'd hate that, I said.

Maida didn't speak—she ate in silence. The wind whistled around us; the distant traffic horned. We'd talked around her for awhile. He asked me about the running shoes we'd bought together the week prior. Were they broken in yet? I spoke of my blistered feet.

That's why you walk so funny.

Fuck off, no I don't.

I want to watch a movie, Maida interjected, flatly. Like, a good one.

It was the first real thing she had said all night.

What about that Damien Chazelle film that's your favorite, Theo. *Whiplash*? Should we all watch it tonight? You haven't seen it, have you Salem?

In the space of the silence, Theo and I shared a look that clearly indicated a knowingness, that we'd seen it together. She caught it in the low light.

Right. Well.

Maida stood up and collected her things. There were still two tacos on her plate.

We should watch it. I'll set it up, Theo tried.

Don't.

She went inside our room and didn't come back out for the rest of the night.

She didn't speak to me for three full days after. I tiptoed around her in common spaces and would always brew enough coffee for the both of us regardless. She always drank it. The dishes piled up and I washed them while she was away. I didn't see much of her those days. She had been sleeping elsewhere. On that last day I remember seeing her in the living room around nine and wondered if she would be staying the whole night. At eleven I climbed into bed, and she lay carefully beside me about an hour later—careful not to make much movement, as if neither of us were there.

I don't want him like you want him, she said suddenly—strained, after thirty minutes of silence. But you have to understand it does feel like you're both replacing me in some ways.

I don't want him, I lied.

She scoffed. It's insulting you think I would believe that.

The room grew eerie. I didn't have a rebuttal.

She continued. I was already having a bad day that day. That just hurt a bit, is all. Don't get bent up about it.

What happened?

She rolled over so I couldn't see her face. She just said, I can't talk about it.

Early April—two weeks after Irene's 26th birthday—she asked me and Maida to come over. I was on the phone with Theo when she texted us. He was on a work trip in New York. I told him I couldn't find my sandals and he said, They're under your bed, are they not? Which, they were.

When we got to Irene's her face was glowing wet and red. Stray black hairs stuck to the tears like a curtain. She told us her boyfriend had broken up with her by way of blocking her number, her socials. When she showed up to his apartment, his housemates wouldn't open the door.

I don't understand, she said. I don't get it.

Maida said something similar happened to a friend from back home, and I said I'd heard about this sort of thing from a cousin. We brought her back to our place—to rest in a bed he hadn't been in—and she slept in between the two of us. We all held each other very close. That night, all the minor tremors and shakes of her grieving body were mimicked by mine as well.

The night Theo returned from his trip, I picked him up from the airport in his car—he left me the keys. When he got in he grabbed my hand briefly, squeezed it, and said, God. I missed you. My nerves unraveled. Then this hand was his again.

When we walked into his house, I'd had Chinese food I ordered set out already. We talked about what we had done in each other's absence. When he asked if I'd been over at all, I told him I had been. That sometimes I would sleep there just because. You must like me a lot to do something like that, he said. I told him he must like me a lot to allow me.

Your house is so normal, I said, looking around.

What's wrong with my house?

Nothing. It just strikes me as odd you have the means for nice things, but you live relatively normally. You have a normal car, too.

First my house, now my car… he teased. He ran his foot alongside my calf under the table.

You know what I mean.

I have nice things, Salem. Just because they're not extravagant doesn't mean they're not nice.

This is not a criticism, Theodore. It's an observation. My God.

I used my foot to touch him back. The sound of his embarrassed laugh put me on the verge of collapse. In that moment, I wanted to kiss him more than I wanted to live.

After dinner, after wine, I told him an anecdote from the day prior. I'd been on my same running path, and a guy I saw a lot stopped me to say hi. We talked for thirty minutes, and at the end he asked me if I'd let him take me out.

He shifted on the couch a bit.

And what did you say? He asked, not entirely indifferent.

I said, let me think about it.

I wanted to catch his eye, to read him, but he wouldn't let me. His aloofness was as alarming as his beauty, which was already profound. I could feel the retreat.

Theo played with his watch, then scratched his head, then played with the dial once more. Tan hands searching for something to attend to. Casually, while looking out the window he said:

You should do it. You should be happy.

Should I? I said tightly.

He nodded, then finally met my eyes. They were definitive. I remember this feeling, I thought.

I asked him if he was happy, which meant more than just that. After a long while he said, Happy enough.

I told him I was glad and that I should probably head out.

I stood up and he let me. I went for the door and he let me.

When I got home the door slammed hard behind me. Maida called from the other room asking me what was wrong at the exact time I said, Will it always be like this?

What do you mean? She asked.

I stood very still by the door. I said, I think I'm wired wrong.

Salem, she said, You're scaring me. She brought a palm to my face and dragged me to the couch. What are you talking about?

New York spilled from my lips—jagged, fragmented. It was a storm of a cry. She nodded through the debris. My boogers salted my molars, but what could I do. Maida's arms were so tight around me I felt I might be permanently dented. God, she said. Why would you keep this from me?

I told her that the worst part was that I knew the whole time. I would hold his face in my hands, and it felt like the sheer magnetism of the closeness of our bodies could pull tears from my eyes. I could cry just looking at him. When we kissed my lips were charged for hours. I am not being hyperbolic—it was a full body sensation. I knew the entire time we lived together he did not feel that way about me, and I stayed anyways. What an embarrassing thing to admit, I said. What a horribly, degrading thing to feel.

When my body's shutter began to slow, she told me that she had been seeing River since December, but that River wanted to keep it a secret.

We fight about it a lot. Her eyes were empty and cold. They said they're not ready to commit to something again, Maida said. That telling our friends would pressure them to commit, and they didn't want me to resent them.

We shared a long, aching look that twisted in my chest. I wondered if anyone knew what they were doing.

In bed that night we held hands.

I wish you'd told me that sooner. She said this barely audible. It all makes more sense now. Is that what's stopping you? You think it's happening again?

We turned and found each other's eyes in the darkness, letting our sight adjust.

I keep making the same mistakes.

Until you don't. She squeezed my hand.

Sometimes, I think I will be this miserable and alone forever. That I'll die never having felt anything returned. Not once in all my life.

Salem, her voice broke. You're only twenty-five.

Which, I knew. But it was the oldest I'd ever been.

In the morning the sun was there. Traffic clogged. The world carried on. Maida went to have brunch with River. Irene hadn't talked to anyone in a day or two. I had six missed calls from Theo and a text that said: Come see me tonight.

There was no wine that night. It was the clearest I'd been in months. I watched Theo's tall frame move about in the low light of the kitchen—languid, anxious. He was playing *God's Favorite Customer* in full, probably to tug at me.

I realized last night that I find it embarrassing to have feelings for someone.

I said this very low and slow, with no regard to whether he was listening or not.

Probably, I continued, because I've never experienced the feeling returned in full. But then I started thinking—is it so wrong to always care for someone more than they care for you? Like, what happens if you just embrace it and say—yes, I am totally yours. I am totally under your control. I don't care what you do to me because if it's what you want, it's what I want, and I want to have the things I want to have.

Theo had stopped doing whatever it was he was doing at that point, but he didn't look at me.

I'm not totally convinced by my own point, I said. That this is an okay thing. Especially if the person knows their power over you. But when you really adore someone, you want what they want, and if you're working on their terms I suppose that's only the case because you allow it—does that make it your terms as well? Do they really have power over you or are you just *allowing* them to think have power over you? You just as easily could say, I'm consumed by you, but I know I care about you more than you care about me, and it hurts, so I'm just going to go. But instead, you stay, so—isn't that all within your agency? I'm not sure if I'm making sense, I said, shy, folding my hands into my lap. I think we all just want to be loved by the people we love so there's no fuss about any of this stuff. If I had that I don't think I'd be thinking about all this so hard.

He analyzed me like an equation.

You're not usually like this, he said. So forward.

You don't like me like this.

No, no. I always like you.

Well, I said. It occurred to me last night I may just be a desperate person as well.

Do you really think you care about me more than I care about you?

I shrugged. You might. You might not. I don't know what it looks like.

Do you know what I think?

What do you think, Theodore?

With a smile he said, I think Maida was right. We are both stubborn. He took a sip of water, and then said, I also think that not having you around would destroy me as a person.

I don't believe you.

It's true. Actually, on my trip, there was a moment where I expected you in my hotel room. Not literally, but in feeling. I've been Pavloved into expecting you at the end of the day. When I sat there in my bed I thought, I just want to go home. Then you called me asking where your sandals were. I thought, I could never forgive myself if I fucked this up. If I was selfish with you. But at the same time, I'm selfish enough to imagine what that world would look like. Maybe I haven't learned anything at all.

I thought of something I'd read about knowing your condition and acting foolish despite that awareness, but my nerves were too wound for cleverness.

You know that first night, when you held me while I was crying, I almost bit your neck.

He laughed. Why didn't you?

Because I realized you're just nice. I can't keep wanting people just because they're nice to me.

I need you to accept that some people might just desire you. There isn't always a catch.

Some people? I joking raised my eyebrows. Do you know these people? I do.

And they told you that? That they desire me?

They did.

When our silence reclaimed the room, I remembered music was playing. "We Are Only People (And There's Not Much Anyone Can Do About That)" began to play, slowly. The last song on *God's Favorite Customer*.

We didn't speak the entire time it played—I knew it was his favorite song. Theo stood on the other side of the room. Black hair in his face, jaw tense. I felt a familiar feeling. It was making home in my chest. We didn't look away the entire time. Not through the chorus, the verses. The slow burn at its start. The swell in the middle. I could feel the soundwaves in my spine. I might've cried. We held that gaze until the very final moments, into the slowing instrumentation, the falling action; through the final line as Misty fervidly, desperately moaned: Why not you, Why not me, Why not now?

Is that what you want, he asked me in the newly hushed room.

I couldn't move.

If that's what you want.

I want what you want.

I looked at him and he looked at me. I thought about the warmth of his neck but in his hand, and not on my nose but on my leg.

My body was a furnace.

I thought, maybe it is happening again. Or maybe it isn't. It didn't matter. We reached for each other at the same time.

ACKNOWLEDGMENTS

I owe a tremendous thanks to my mother and my father, who had been privy to my desire to be a writer since I was a child and never once attempted to deter me. Had they not pushed me to follow this desire wholeheartedly and to depths far outside my comfort zone, this collection would not exist. To my brother Lee for always believing in me and loving me—taking care of me, inspiring me. Your support and enthusiasm truly has always meant the world to me. Thank you to my two dear friends—extensions of myself—Mary Kate and Samantha. You've read every single thing I've written over the last eleven years. I cannot imagine the process of writing without you to turn to. What would I do without the constant presence of your love? Everything I know about friendship; you have taught me.

I am thankful to all of my instructors at the University of Kentucky as well as my peers for workshopping some of these stories and helping me push them into the right direction. To Dr. DaMaris Hill—for supporting me in a difficult time, which allowed me to write the final four stories of this collection. To Crystal Wilkinson, for your support and guidance on a number of these stories as an instructor, the chair of my committee, and a mentor.

I've been writing my entire life and have shown my writing to *so* many people throughout middle school, high school, college and beyond. You all know who you are. I am deeply indebted and would not be here without every single last one of you. Thank you to everyone at Four Way Books and Kimbilio for this opportunity. David Haynes, for your edits, your kind words. Thank you to Deesha Philyaw for selecting this collection and giving it a life.

Henry—there are not words in the English language to describe how incredible you are, and how incredible you have been. The extent of your love, kindness, and support never ceases to amaze me. Thank you for reaching for me at the same time.

And thank you, reader, for your time.

ABOUT THE AUTHOR

Allegra Solomon was born and raised in Columbus, Ohio. She got her MFA from the University of Kentucky and her B.A. in Creative Writing from Ohio University. Her work has been nominated for the Pushcart Prize, Best of the Net, and has appeared in *The Georgia Review, American Literary Review, New Ohio Review, Lolwe, The Account,* and more. In 2023, *There's Nothing Left For You Here* won the Kimbilio National Fiction Prize. This is her first book.

PUBLICATION OF THIS BOOK WAS MADE POSSIBLE
BY GRANTS AND DONATIONS. WE ARE ALSO GRATEFUL
TO THOSE INDIVIDUALS WHO PARTICIPATED IN
OUR BUILD A BOOK PROGRAM. THEY ARE:

Anonymous (14), Robert Abrams, Debra Allbery, Nancy Allen,
Michael Ansara, Kathy Aponick, Jean Ball, Sally Ball, Jill Bialosky,
Sophie Cabot Black, Laurel Blossom, Tommye Blount,
Karen and David Blumenthal, Jonathan Blunk, Lee Briccetti,
Jane Martha Brox, Mary Lou Buschi, Anthony Cappo,
Carla and Steven Carlson, Robin Rosen Chang, Liza Charlesworth,
Peter Coyote, Elinor Cramer, Kwame Dawes,
Michael Anna de Armas, Brian Komei Dempster,
Renko and Stuart Dempster, Matthew DeNichilo, Rosalynde Vas Dias,
Patrick Donnelly, Charles R. Douthat, Lynn Emanuel, Blas Falconer,
Laura Fjeld, Carolyn Forché, Helen Fremont and Donna Thagard,
Debra Gitterman, Dorothy Tapper Goldman, Alison Granucci,
Elizabeth T. Gray Jr., Naomi Guttman and Jonathan Mead,
Jeffrey Harrison, KT Herr, Carlie Hoffman, Melissa Hotchkiss,
Thomas and Autumn Howard, Catherine Hoyser, Elizabeth Jackson,
Linda Susan Jackson, Jessica Jacobs, Deborah Jonas-Walsh, Jennifer Just,
Voki Kalfayan, Maeve Kinkead, Victoria Korth, David Lee and
Jamila Trindle, Rodney Terich Leonard, Howard Levy, Owen Lewis and
Susan Ennis, Eve Linn, Matthew Lippman, Ralph and Mary Ann Lowen,
Maja Lukic, Neal Lulofs, Anthony Lyons, Ricardo Alberto Maldonado,
Trish Marshall, Donna Masini, Deborah McAlister, Carol Moldaw,
Michael and Nancy Murphy, Kimberly Nunes, Matthew Olzmann and
Vievee Francis, Veronica Patterson, Patrick Phillips, Robert Pinsky,
Megan Pinto, Kevin Prufer, Anna Duke Reach, Paula Rhodes,
Yoana Setzer, James Shalek, Soraya Shalforoosh, Peggy Shinner,
Joan Silber, Jane Simon, Debra Spark, Donna Spruijt-Metz,

Arlene Stang, Page Hill Starzinger, Catherine Stearns, Yerra Sugarman, Arthur Sze, Laurence Tancredi, Marjorie and Lew Tesser, Peter Turchi, Connie Voisine, Susan Walton, Martha Webster and Robert Fuentes, Calvin Wei, Allison Benis White, Lauren Yaffe, and Rolf Yngve.